Five Nights at Freddy's™

TALES FROM THE PIZZAPLEX

#2 HAPPS

BY

SCOTT CAWTHON
ELLEY COOPER
ANDREA WAGGENER

Scholastic Inc.

First published by Scholastic in the US, 2022
This edition published by Scholastic in the UK, 2022
Euston House, 24 Eversholt Street, London, NW1 1DB
Scholastic Ireland, 89E Lagan Road, Dublin Industrial Estate, Glasnevin,
Dublin, D11 HP5F

SCHOLASTIC and associated logos are trademarks and/or
registered trademarks of Scholastic Inc.

Text © Scott Cawthon, 2022

ISBN 978 1338 83169 6

A CIP catalogue record for this book is available from the British Library.

Printed in the UK by CPI Group UK (Ltd), Croydon, CR0 4YY
Paper made from wood grown in sustainable forests and other controlled sources.

1 3 5 7 9 10 8 6 4 2

www.scholastic.co.uk

Five Nights at Freddy's

TALES FROM THE PIZZAPLEX

#2 HAPPS

TABLE OF CONTENTS

HELP
WANTED

WHY IS THE MEN'S ROOM ALWAYS SUCH A NIGHT-MARE? STEVE SPRAYED THE TOILET AND WALLS WITH DISINFECTANT. IT WAS WEIRD. THE WOMEN'S ROOM NEVER NEEDED ANYTHING BUT A BASIC MOP, WIPE-DOWN, AND REPLENISHING OF SOAP AND TOILET PAPER. BUT WHEN TAKING CARE OF THE MEN'S ROOM, HE ALWAYS FELT LIKE HE MIGHT AS WELL BE CLEANING THE MONKEY HOUSE AT THE ZOO.

Steve never thought he'd be scrubbing toilets at a gas station for minimum wage. With his digital art and design skills, he always figured he'd be working for one of the many tech companies in his booming city, prefer-ably designing video games. He had a billion ideas, many of them better than games that were already on the mar-ket, if he did say so himself.

Yet here he was, with a toilet brush in one hand and a bottle of spray cleaner in the other.

For the past several years, he had applied for any posi-tion at a tech company that he was remotely qualified for. But the competition was fierce. He was up against all these kids with expensive Ivy League degrees who had already done internships or had jobs at the most prestigious companies in the country. Steve had graduated from a local public college, paying for his tuition by working long hours at crappy jobs. And once he earned his degree, he was never hired for anything but more crappy jobs. He made his way to the second stall in the men's room. In this case, the term *crappy job* was literal.

Steve's tiny studio apartment was one floor above a take-out place called Cap'n Ernie's Fish Boat. The greasy odor wafted upward so that the carpet, furniture, and bedding in the apartment always smelled of fried fish. Even Steve's clothes hanging in the closet had absorbed the smell. Sometimes stray cats followed him on the street, breathing in his fishy aroma.

As soon as Steve got home from work, a shower was absolutely essential. Sometimes he felt like he should spray himself with the disinfectant he used to clean the gas station restrooms. By the time he showered and changed into clean, comfortable—if slightly fishy-smelling—clothes, he was ready to eat something and get to his real work. He popped a frozen burrito in the microwave, grabbed a soda from the fridge, and sat down at the computer.

The project he was working on, *Chip Off the Old Block*, was a family-friendly fetch quest–based game featuring cartoony chipmunks. He was about halfway through the design, and he hoped that a company would be interested in it. But if they weren't, maybe he'd try to just bring it out himself. He was tired of cleaning toilets and waiting for something to happen.

Which reminded him. He should message Amanda before it was past her bedtime.

Recently, Steve's tiredness of waiting for something to happen had led him to join a dating app. He had always dreamed of marrying a smart, kind, beautiful woman. They would live in a comfortable house and have two adorable kids, a boy and a girl. But dreams were one thing, reality was another.

Strangely, one didn't meet many attractive women cleaning toilets and mopping floors at a gas station convenience store. Occasionally, an interesting woman would come into the store to pay for gas or grab a gallon of milk, but it was hard to be suave with a mop in your hand.

For a while, he didn't think he was going to meet anyone through the app, either. But then he had seen Amanda's profile and sent her a cautious message that only said "hi." She said "hi" back almost immediately. After that, they progressed to an actual conversation. Well, as close to an actual conversation as texting could be.

Steve had been drawn to Amanda's profile pic not just because she was traditionally beautiful but because she seemed to radiate kindness. She had shoulder-length brown hair and a winning smile. She was a preschool teacher, and Steve figured she was a good one because of her kindness, patience, and sense of humor. The weird thing about their relationship was that even though they had been chatting for over a month, they had gone out on only two real dates. Steve worked at the gas station from 3:00 p.m. until 10:00 p.m., and Amanda worked at the preschool from 7:30 a.m. until 3:30 p.m. They couldn't have found more incompatible schedules if they had tried.

Steve grabbed his phone and texted her, *I hope you had a good day.*

She texted back, *A kid threw up on my shoes first thing this morning but at least my day had to get better from there LOL.*

Steve chuckled. He guessed they both had to deal with more than their fair share of grossness at their jobs. He typed *LOL if things went downhill from there it would be pretty bad. I'll let you get some rest. Good night.*

She texted back *night night* with a sleepy face emoji.

Steve smiled, set aside his phone, and settled back in to work on his game until he was too tired to stay awake anymore.

★ ★ ★

As soon as Steve opened the door of the convenience store, his manager, a humorless, middle-aged man with the unfortunate name of Gilbert Hurlbutt, looked up from his phone and said, "Some kid spilled about a gallon of blue slushie over by the back left cooler. Go mop it up."

"No problem," Steve said, which was what he always said to Mr. Hurlbutt. It was the path of least resistance.

He went to the janitorial closet and set the mop bucket under the faucet in the utility sink. Would it have killed Mr. Hurlbutt to say hello before he started barking orders? Steve poured some cleaning solution into the filling bucket and thought, not for the first time, about the bizarreness of Mr. Hurlbutt's name. Mr. Hurlbutt's parents, presumably Mr. Hurlbutt Senior and Mrs. Hurlbutt, knew that they were having a child who would be saddled with their ridiculous last name. So why not give the kid a normal name like Matthew or David or something instead of saddling him with an equally unwieldy first name? Of course, that being said, Mr. Hurlbutt could choose to go by Gil or Bert, but instead the name GILBERT was stitched right over the breast pocket of his uniform shirt.

Steve's wandering thoughts resulted in the mop bucket overflowing. He tilted it and poured out some of the excess water, then carried the bucket and mop to the back of the store to clean up the sticky mess.

Steve's hands were mopping, but his mind was on his game and what he would work on as soon as he got home from this meaningless job.

"I said, can you spare me a moment?"

Steve had been so preoccupied he hadn't even noticed that a man was standing right next to him trying to get his attention. The man in question did not resemble the customers they usually got in the store—exhausted, inexpensively dressed people coming from or going to night-shift jobs. Even though Steve didn't know much about clothes, he could tell this man's dark suit was expensive. It was spotless and wrinkle free and seemed to have been tailored to the contours of his body. "I'm sorry. Can I help you?" Steve said.

"I think perhaps you can," the man said. He had strong, chiseled features and a haircut that looked as expensive as his suit. "That is, if you're Steve Snodgrass."

"I am," Steve said, pointing to his name tag and immediately feeling like an idiot.

"Could you step outside with me for a moment?" the man asked.

This situation was getting stranger and stranger. Steve had thought the man just needed help locating an item in the store, but now it appeared that this guy wanted something from him personally. Steve felt nervous. Was the guy a cop? A serial killer?

"I don't know about that, sir," Steve said. "I just started my shift, so I'm not due for a break yet. I don't want to get in trouble with my boss."

"Well, if you'll step outside with me, you may find yourself working for another boss and for a great deal more money." He smiled. His teeth were perfect.

Steve was growing more confused by the moment. Was this man in the Mafia? "I'm afraid I don't understand."

"Perhaps this will help," the man said, handing Steve a business card.

Steve looked down at the card and read:

> *Brock Edwards*
> *Talent Acquisition*
> *Fazbear Entertainment*

It took a few seconds for the name *Fazbear* to ring a bell. But then Steve remembered the kids' pizza places that had once been wildly popular but had suffered a downfall after a variety of criminal allegations. There had been talk of murders, though Steve didn't remember how many. There was weirder stuff, too . . . stories about paranormal events and that kind of nonsense. Steve was still puzzled, but he had to admit he was curious, too. "Maybe I could step outside for just one minute," he said.

"Very good, Mr. Snodgrass," Mr. Edwards said, following Steve out the back door.

They stood out back near the dumpster. The fumes of garbage hung in the air.

"You are familiar with Fazbear Entertainment?" Mr. Edwards asked.

"Kind of," Steve said. "I mean, I went to the pizza place a couple of times as a kid. Birthday parties and that kind of thing. And also, I know a little about the . . . scandals."

"Unfortunately, that's what a lot of people know about Fazbear Entertainment," Mr. Edwards said. "Over the past few years, there have been a number of individuals determined to smear our company's reputation by spreading terrible rumors. And of course the public dines on that kind of filth." He straightened his already-straight tie. "And so as a result, Fazbear Entertainment is in need of some rebranding."

"Okay, but I still don't see what this has to do with me."

Mr. Edwards looked Steve up and down. "You are a game designer, are you not?"

"An aspiring one, I guess you could say." How did this guy know he made games?

"You sell yourself short, Mr. Snodgrass. You've posted two games online, and they were quite good."

"Thanks," Steve said, though he still wasn't sure how this guy had found out about his games. He wondered what else Brock Edwards knew about him.

"And so here's where you come in," Mr. Edwards said. "In an effort to laugh off our detractors, Fazbear Entertainment wants to put out a line of video games based on the lies that have been spread about the company. Horror games."

"You mean like horror games based on what people say happened in the old pizza places?" Steve said. The idea seemed distasteful at best, cruel at worst.

"Yes," Mr. Edwards said. "They should be scary, but at the same time, they should poke fun at the ridiculousness of all those libelous rumors and accusations." He put on a smile that looked calculated. "We'd like you to develop a series of four games for us, Mr. Snodgrass. I think you'd find the compensation much more generous than what you're currently being paid for . . . er, mopping."

A job offer in game development. It was what Steve had dreamed of his entire life. So why did it feel so weird and wrong?

"We'd want you to start right away, of course. We would fly you to a remote location where you'd have everything you'd need to work on the game, plus everything you'd need to live comfortably: a spacious condominium, personal chef, staff to run your errands and do your laundry. A home gym . . . if you choose to use it." He looked disdainfully at Steve's gym-free physique. "We could give you until Friday to tie up any loose ends. It's an incredible opportunity, Mr. Snodgrass. What do you say?"

"Horror games, huh?" Steve said, stalling. If they were horror games based on ghosts and goblins or other purely fictional creatures, he wouldn't have a problem with them. But horror games based on what he had understood to be real murders made him feel queasy. Fazbear Entertainment said the murders weren't real, but they *would* say that, wouldn't they?

"That's right," Mr. Edwards said. "They'd need to be based in the Fazbear Entertainment universe, but you'd have a lot of creative freedom within those bounds."

"But I couldn't work on them here?" There was something troubling about this whole situation that he couldn't quite put his finger on.

"No, the company was very specific about that. They don't want any chance of leaks."

Leaving town for a long period of time was another sticking point. It was hard enough to see Amanda given their differing work schedules. They hadn't gotten close enough yet to make a long-distance relationship work. He was starting to think he really liked her. If he took a chance with Fazbear Entertainment, a company with a dicey reputation at best, was it worth the risk of losing his chance with Amanda?

"I truly appreciate the offer, Mr. Edwards, but I just don't feel right about taking this job. The world's a scary enough place without adding more horror to it. I really want to concentrate on making family-friendly games." He had his personal reasons for saying no as well, but this was probably the biggest one. Didn't kids already have enough to be scared of in today's world?

Mr. Edwards laughed for a longer time than was comfortable. "Do you mean to tell me that you're going to walk away from this opportunity, go back inside that store, and pick up that mop?"

"Yes, I do," Steve said. "But thank you for your offer."

He wasn't looking forward to going back inside, getting yelled at by Mr. Hurlbutt, and cleaning the floors and the toilets. But somehow he still felt strangely good about his decision.

Still in his pajamas, Steve padded barefoot in the kitchen to start a pot of coffee. A little something to eat and some major caffeine, and he'd be ready to settle in and work on *Chip Off the Old Block* for a few hours until it was time to head to the Gas Up. He popped some bread into the toaster and grabbed a couple of eggs from the fridge.

★ ★ ★

His phone pinged.

Thinking it might be Amanda, he picked it up. Someone had messaged him on the dating app. Strange. It definitely wasn't Amanda because she would've just sent him a regular text. Curiosity got the better of him. He opened the app and saw *A message from Victoria.*

Who the heck was Victoria?

He opened the message and read: *Hi. Would you like to chat sometime?*

He clicked on her picture to enlarge it. When he saw it, he gasped. If someone had asked him to describe what his physical ideal of a woman would be, his description would exactly match the photo he was looking at. Victoria had long, wavy black hair with a beautiful sheen that caught the light. She had big, doe-like brown eyes and a sun-kissed complexion. Her cheekbones were high, and her lips were full. She wore just enough makeup to accentuate her natural beauty.

Of course, he reminded himself, people were notoriously dishonest on the internet. This could be a random photo that someone much less physically attractive had found to pass off as their own. Or it could be a photo of the actual woman from twenty years ago.

But what if it wasn't—what if this vision of loveliness was real and had decided, for whatever reason, that she was interested in him?

Wait, he told himself. *What about Amanda?*

Amanda was a nice, caring person, and there seemed to be a real connection between them. But then again, they were in such an early stage of their relationship that he wasn't even sure it could be called a relationship yet. And they hadn't said they were exclusive. Amanda could be dating half a dozen other guys for all he knew.

He hit "reply" to Victoria's message and typed one word: *Sure.*

As soon as he tapped "send," Steve smelled something burning. It was like for a few minutes there, he had entirely lost track of where he was and what he was doing. *Home. Kitchen. Breakfast,* he reminded himself. He looked at the counter and saw black smoke rolling from the toaster.

After he threw away the burnt toast, opened a window to let the smoke out, and poured himself a cup of coffee, Steve sat down at the computer to work on his game. The mysterious message from Victoria, whoever she might be, had left him too keyed up to feel like eating anything.

His phone pinged again.

Victoria: Hi. It's me. I'm glad you said you'd like to chat. Is now a good time?

Sure, Steve typed. Any time's a good time. As soon as the words appeared on the screen, Steve did a face-palm. So much for not sounding too eager.

Victoria: I've never used a dating app before. I'm really more of a face-to-face person. Would you like to meet sometime soon. Maybe this weekend?
Steve: Sure.

Victoria: You could come to my house if you want. It's out in the country. It's really quiet. We'd have plenty of privacy to talk and get to know each other.

Steve: Are you sure you want me to come to your house for our first meeting? Shouldn't we meet in a public place first in case I'm a creep or something?

Victoria: LOL I trust you. How about Saturday at noon? I'll make us lunch.

Steve: Sounds great.

As soon as they finished chatting, Steve remembered he had plans with Amanda for Saturday. She was an understanding person, though. She'd be okay with rescheduling. He texted her, *So sorry but something came up can't do Saturday*. Almost immediately, she texted back *Disappointed but OK* with a sad emoji.

Steve felt guilty, but he told himself he'd make it up to her.

Matt, still dressed in the uniform of the computer store he managed, dunked a doughnut in his coffee. "But I thought things were going good with Amanda," he said.

"They are." Steve had called Matt asking if he could meet him at the all-night doughnut shop after work. His life was getting way too eventful all of a sudden, and Matt, his best friend since freshman year of college, was the only person he felt like he could talk to about it. Matt was unfailingly honest and had never hesitated to tell Steve when he was making a horrible mistake. (Matt also seemed to have the infuriating habit of always being right.) "But this message," Steve said, "it came out of nowhere, and this woman—" Suddenly, he was at a loss for words.

"This woman said she'd send goons to beat the crap out of you if you didn't go out with her?"

Steve laughed. "No."

"This woman said if you didn't go out with her, she'd make all your darkest secrets a matter of public record?"

"No," Steve said, still laughing. "But to be fair, my life to date has been too boring to accumulate many dark secrets." He took a deep breath and tried to find the words to explain himself. "This woman—" He picked up his phone. "Here, let me show you." He opened up the dating app, found Victoria's picture, and showed it to Matt.

Matt's jaw dropped, and so did his doughnut. "Whoa," he said. "I get it. I totally get it."

Steve handed him another doughnut. He was relieved that Matt understood.

Even though he was beginning to doubt his GPS, Steve turned off a narrow, winding country road onto another narrow, winding country road. It was beautiful out here, with rolling hills and trees and the occasional pasture full of cows, but Steve couldn't imagine living somewhere so remote. He also couldn't imagine that a woman as beautiful and glamorous as Victoria would want to live in such a rural area. Surely someone so lovely and charming would want to live where she could see and be seen.

"Turn left on Brushy Pine Road," the GPS ordered. "Your destination will be on your left."

The destination seemed to be a long gravel driveway that led into a densely wooded area. Steve drove doubtfully, but the GPS had never steered him wrong before.

Finally, the driveway ended at a house. It was small and modest, a neat little white cottage with green shutters and a green front door. It looked more like a home for someone's grandmother than for an attractive, young, single woman. He parked, grabbed the bouquet of grocery-store flowers he had selected for her, and walked up to knock on the door.

No one answered. Steve sighed. Had this been some kind of trick?

He tried the door and was surprised to find it unlocked. "Hello? Anybody home?" he called. When there was no response, he stepped inside. He wouldn't normally have entered someone's house without permission, but he reasoned that he had been invited and that was good enough.

Steve was surprised to find himself standing in an empty room. The white walls were blank, the windows were curtainless, and there was not a single piece of furniture in sight. He wondered if he had made some kind of mistake. Was she meeting him as a real estate agent trying to sell him a house instead of as a date?

The house may have been empty, but it was not silent. There was a soft but steady mechanical whirring sound, and then, so suddenly that it made Steve jump, a loud, high-pitched ringing that hurt his ears, his brain.

What was going on in this bizarre place? He felt suddenly unsteady on his feet and propped himself up against the wall to regain his balance.

"Steve!" The horrible ringing stopped and was replaced by a voice like velvet. "I'm so sorry. I must not have heard the door." Her looks did not disappoint. She was just like the picture online except better because she was standing there right in front of him. She was wearing a formfitting green dress, which complemented the flecks of green in her brown eyes. Her figure was fit and toned, as if she worked out regularly, but was also curvy in the right places.

Steve was instantly besotted. "Hi," he said, wishing he had planned some kind of clever opening line. Since he hadn't, he shoved the bouquet at her instead.

She received the flowers and smiled, all lovely lips and straight white teeth. "How beautiful . . . and thoughtful, too! Thank you." She looked around the room as if trying to imagine it from his point of view. "I know I haven't done much with the place yet, but with the right touches, I think it'll be really cozy. And for our lunch, I thought we could have sort of a picnic on the floor. We can put down a blanket, and I have bread and cheese and fruit and some good chocolate."

"That sounds nice." Before Steve could say anything else, there was another horrible, high-pitched electronic scream. He looked up in the direction of the sound and saw the red light flashing on the smoke alarm. It was strange. He could neither see nor smell smoke. He reached up to try to disable it but lost his footing as the room began to spin faster and faster like an out-of-control merry-go-round.

Steve opened his eyes. He was lying on a couch, but where? The layout of the small room was familiar, but when he had seen it before, it had been empty. Now there was the chocolate-brown couch he was lying on and a matching armchair. There was a coffee table stacked with both fashion magazines and tech-themed magazines and a large cabinet with a flat-screen TV and a few different kinds of video game consoles. The walls that had been blank before were now hung with photos of Victoria. Victoria hiking in the mountains, her lustrous hair windblown and beautiful. Victoria, tan and toned and gorgeous in an emerald-green, two-piece swimsuit, lounging on the beach. Victoria eating an ice-cream cone on a park bench, looking adorable with a dab of ice cream on her perfect nose.

Victoria herself came padding barefoot into the room, wearing jeans and a black fitted T-shirt. Hadn't she been wearing a dress earlier? Then again, the room had been empty earlier, too. Steve was hopelessly confused and disoriented.

"Hey, babe," Victoria said. "You had a bad dizzy spell and kind of passed out on the couch. I brought you a glass of water. Why don't you try to sit up and drink a little?"

Steve had never had a dizzy spell before, but now that he thought about it, he had been too nervous about the date to eat breakfast this morning. He sat up slowly. "You know, I think maybe I need to eat something." He accepted the water glass and was surprised to find himself drinking it down in a few gulps. "Weren't we going to have a picnic on the floor?"

Now Victoria looked confused. "A picnic on the floor? You mean, like on our first date?"

"Our first date? But isn't this—" Steve looked around the furnished room. "I'm sorry. I'm really confused."

Victoria sat down next to him and took his hand. Confused or not, Steve loved having her close to him. Touching him.

"It happens, honey. It happens," she said, squeezing his hand. "Sometimes you forget things. You have memory loss as a result of that car accident you had a few years ago."

"I don't remember a car accident," Steve said. He was a very careful driver.

"Exactly." Victoria squeezed his knee. "You took a bad hit on the head. Brain injury. Most of the time you're fine, but sometimes your memory just wipes temporarily. And then it's like you reset, and you're all good again."

This was upsetting news. He wondered how many times Victoria had had to tell it to him. "But I always reset so I remember things again?"

Victoria smiled. "Always."

Steve nodded. The explanation was weird, but it also made sense. His sense of time was off. That explained everything. "So you and I . . . we're together?"

Victoria laughed. "We are very, very together. Wait." She got up from the couch, grabbed one of the framed pictures off the wall, and handed it to him.

The photo was taken outdoors under an arch of flowers. Victoria stood smiling in a lacy white gown and veil, holding a bouquet of flowers that matched the ones decorating the arch. Steve was standing beside her in a tux, but the main thing he was wearing was an impossibly big smile.

No wonder, Steve thought. His wedding day had to have been the happiest day of his life. Too bad he had no memory of it whatsoever. "You're so beautiful," he said.

"It was a beautiful dress," Victoria said.

"Not just in the picture," Steve said. "Always. You're always so beautiful."

"Aww, you're too sweet to me," Victoria said. She leaned forward and pressed her lips to his.

It was wonderful. It felt like their first kiss.

★ ★ ★

"Daddy! Wake up! It's time for pancakes!"

Steve opened his eyes. Two children were standing beside the bed. They were wearing pajamas with some kind of cartoon characters on them and jumping up and down and yelling, "Pancakes! Pancakes!" The girl looked to be around four and the boy around two. Both of them had thick black hair and big brown, green-flecked eyes. They were beautiful children. The girl and boy he had always wanted. But he had no memory of pregnancies, of births, of infancies or childhoods before this moment. He didn't even know the kids' names. Were they his?

"Pancakes, huh?" he said, sitting up in bed and trying

in vain to orient himself. The walls, he noticed, were covered with photos of the children, from babyhood until now. Steve was even in some of the pictures with them.

"Today is Saturday, and on Saturday Mommy always makes pancakes," the little girl said like she was lecturing him.

"Okay, sounds good," Steve said, standing up. "Lead the way."

The little girl took one of his hands, and the little boy took the other. It was a sweet, unfamiliar feeling, those tiny hands gripping his.

Victoria was in the kitchen, looking beautiful even in her pink bathrobe with no makeup and her hair unstyled. She was standing over a skillet, expertly flipping pancakes.

"All hail the Pancake Queen," Steve said, kissing her on the cheek.

"Pancake Wench is more like it," she said, laughing. "I always forget what a long process this is until I'm actually doing it."

"Well, we appreciate it, don't we, kids?" Steve said. He guessed he'd just call them "kids" until he got a clue about what their names were.

"Thank you, Mommy!" the kids said, hugging her.

"You're very welcome," she said. "Now Abigail and Avery, if you'd take your seats at the table, I'll have your pancakes ready in a minute." She turned to Steve. "And honey, the coffee's ready if you'd like to get us some."

"Sure," Steve said, though in his head he was repeating *Abigail and Avery, Abigail and Avery*. He didn't know where the coffee cups were, and he opened the wrong cabinet at first but got it right on the second try. He poured them each a cup.

Victoria said, "Just a splash of milk in mine, remember?"

He didn't remember, but he said, "Of course" and got the milk out of the fridge.

It was a happy breakfast. The pancakes themselves were terrific, and the bacon was crispy the way he liked it. But the best part was sitting around the table as a family, the kids talking and laughing, he and Victoria sharing private smiles. This was what he had always wanted. Did it matter that he didn't remember how he had gotten it? Maybe it didn't. People were always saying to live in the moment, and that's what Steve was doing. You couldn't get hung up on your past if you couldn't remember it.

"So, are you still planning on fixing the leaky faucet in the bathroom today?" Victoria asked.

Steve didn't remember that this was the plan, but he had learned about plumbing from his dad, so he was happy to comply. "I'll certainly give it a shot," he said.

A few minutes later, when Steve came back into the living room after fixing the faucet, Victoria was sitting on the couch in the living room, looking distressed. "We need to talk," she said.

Memory problems aside, Steve still knew that that particular sentence never meant good news. "Okay," he said, sitting down beside her.

She picked up an envelope from the coffee table. "This was in the mail today." She handed it to him.

He took out the letter and read the words *Notice of Foreclosure*. "Wait, what? Is our house being foreclosed on?"

"Apparently so," Victoria said. "We've been underwater financially for a while. I really wanted to stay at home with the kids until they started kindergarten, but if I have to, I guess I'll go back to work."

"Let's not be hasty," Steve said. He knew he was going to feel like an idiot saying what he was going to say next, but he had to ask the question. "Do I . . . have a job?"

"Sure," Victoria said. "You work at the Gas Up."

"Oh," he said. He guessed he hadn't forgotten how to clean toilets.

"But even with you working overtime, the pay there doesn't keep up with the cost of living, especially since the kids came along," Victoria said.

"Well, I'm just going to have to find a better-paying job, then."

Victoria gave him a brave smile. "It would be wonderful if you could."

"Here comes the Tickle Monster!" Steve stretched out his arms and wiggled his fingers. Abigail and Avery ran through the living room, giggling.

"Chase me, Daddy! Chase me!" Avery yelled.

He couldn't get over the small burst of happiness he felt every time one of the kids called him Daddy.

★ ★ ★

He heard it before he saw it. That was how it was with their long gravel driveway. If someone was approaching, you always heard the sound of the wheels on the gravel a few seconds before you saw the car. He saw, looking out the window, that in this case, the car was shiny, black, and expensive-looking.

Unless he had forgotten (which was extremely likely, given his memory problems), they weren't expecting anyone. He wondered if it might be someone who wanted to talk to him about the foreclosure, who might want him to sign some papers making the loss of his family's home official. Steve braced himself for the worst. "Kids," he said, "you should go get washed up. Dinner's soon. Your mom's making spaghetti and meatballs."

"Pasketti and meatballs!" Abigail sang, taking her brother by the hand.

"I like meatballs," Avery said.

They hurried off to wash their hands, leaving Steve to meet his fate.

Steve stepped out onto the porch. The black car came to a stop. A moment later, a man stepped out of it.

It was strange. Steve had forgotten so much, and yet he still remembered this man. The styled hair. The perfect suit. Steve even remembered exactly what it had said on his fancy business card: *Brock Edwards, Talent Acquisition, Fazbear Entertainment.*

The man smiled as he approached. His teeth were dazzling. "Mr. Snodgrass," he said, "we've met before."

"Brock Edwards. Fazbear Entertainment," Steve said, holding out his hand to shake.

"You have a good memory," Mr. Edwards said, taking Steve's offered hand.

"For some things," Steve said. "Would you like to sit on the porch? We could go inside, but I've got a four-year-old and a two-year-old, so I can't guarantee much quiet."

"The porch is perfect," Mr. Edwards said.

Once they were settled in the porch's two rocking chairs, Steve asked, "Can I get you anything to drink? Iced tea? Lemonade?"

"No, thank you," Mr. Edwards said. "Steve, since your memory is so good, I'm sure you remember the offer I made you the last time we met."

Strangely, Steve could remember every detail. The horror games based on the "myths" surrounding Fazbear Entertainment. Now, facing foreclosure, the idea of the games didn't seem quite so objectionable. "I do," he said.

Mr. Edwards nodded. "Well, we here at Fazbear Entertainment want you to know that the offer still stands."

"Can I stay here with my family to work on them?" He remembered that last time the offer had involved relocating to an undisclosed area.

"Yes," Mr. Edwards said. "We want you to work wherever and however you're most comfortable."

Steve's face broke out in a grin. Their house was saved. He didn't hesitate. "I'll take it," he said.

That night in bed, Victoria laid her head on his shoulder. "I can't believe you saved us," she said.

"Fazbear Entertainment saved us," Steve said, though he had to admit her words made him feel good.

"Well, but if you didn't have the talent and skills that Fazbear Entertainment wanted, then we wouldn't have been saved. Therefore, *you* saved us." She planted a kiss on his cheek. "You're my hero."

"Aw, shucks," Steve said. But he had to admit, he did feel pleased with himself.

They held each other close, and Steve fell into a deep sleep.

★ ★ ★

It was coming from the living room. A stomping, rumbling sound. A robber? Their house was so far out in the country, Steve was shocked that someone could find it to rob. He got out of bed and put his phone in the pocket of his robe, prepared to call the police.

But wait. When had he last used his phone? All he could remember was that the last time he tried, it hadn't worked at all.

He was going to have to take matters into his own hands. He was scared, but he had to protect his family. He grabbed the softball bat that was in the closet and marched to the living room as though confident instead of terrified.

Abigail was standing in front of the coffee table and bumping into it repeatedly. Her eyes were blank and staring, seemingly at nothing.

"Sweetie, are you okay?" Steve asked, trying not to sound panicked.

She turned to face him and smiled. "Oh! Hi, Daddy."

"Sweetheart, it's the middle of the night. You should go back to bed."

"Okay, Daddy." She shuffled down the hall and disappeared into her room.

The door to Avery's room was slightly ajar, which was the natural state of all the interior doors in the house. For some reason, none of them would fully close, let alone lock.

Just to make sure his son was okay, Steve peeked into his room. Avery was asleep safe and sound, sprawled out with one foot dangling over the side of the bed like always.

Steve was relieved there had been no intruder, but he was also worried and confused. He propped the softball bat up against the wall and climbed back into bed.

"What are you doing?"

In his anxious state, his wife's voice made him nearly jump out of his skin. He took a deep breath, tried to calm down. "Didn't you hear the noise in the living room?"

"No, I didn't hear anything," Victoria said. "And you know what a light sleeper I am. If there had been a noise, I definitely would have heard it. Maybe you were dreaming."

"No, it was real. When I went into the living room, Abigail was standing there. She looked blank and weird and was bumping into the furniture."

Victoria gave him a patient smile. "Sweetheart, do you remember that the children sleepwalk sometimes? They get it from you. You'll be dreaming wild stuff, saying absurd things, and wandering all over the house. I even caught you wandering around in the yard one night. With you, it's sleepwalking with night terrors. Fortunately, the kids just seem to have gotten the sleepwalking part."

"No," Steve said. "I don't remember any of that." It was so upsetting to not be able to piece his recent past together, to not even remember basic facts about himself and his kids.

"Well, now you know so there's no need to worry." Victoria smiled and patted the empty spot beside her. "Come back to bed."

Steve couldn't sleep. He always had that same sensation, of someone or something inside the house wishing to do him and his family harm. And always Victoria comforted him, reminding him about his history of sleep-walking and night terrors. Often Steve marveled at what an amazing wife she was—always so kind and patient and caring. He figured it couldn't be easy to be married to someone like him who was such a mess all the time.

Mess or not, he was really pouring himself into making the first Fazbear Entertainment game. Since the company agreed to let Steve work at home, he had turned the house's tiny attic into his office. He called his daily climbing of the ladder his "commute to work." It was nice to hear Victoria and the children talking and playing beneath him when he was working, and to know that at lunchtime all he had to do was climb down the ladder to join them.

He was still haunted by the nighttime visions and fears, but during the day, he channeled all those feelings into the game he was creating. Those feelings of being unsafe all ended up on the screen in front of him. If Fazbear Entertainment wanted a scary game, then a scary game was what they were going to have.

When Steve climbed down the ladder for lunch, Abigail said, "Surprise, Daddy! We're having a picnic!"

A voice on the radio that Victoria kept on during the day said, "Heavy thunder showers expected over the next twenty-four hours. Take shelter if possible, folks. Lightning is dangerous!"

"It doesn't sound like picnic weather," Steve said.

Victoria, who was carrying a pitcher of lemonade, laughed. "I thought we'd have a picnic indoors. Like our first date."

The picnic was nice. Victoria spread a blanket on the floor, and they ate chicken salad sandwiches and grapes and drank lemonade. After they ate, Abigail said, "Daddy, let's play hide-and-seek!"

"Hide! Seek!" Avery yelled.

Steve knew if he played with them a while, he might tire them out so they would take a nap and give their mom a break. "Sure," he said. "I can play a few rounds before I have to get back to work."

The kids jumped up and down in a frenzy of delight. Steve felt his heart fill with love. They were such adorable, amazing kids. He wished he could remember every minute he had spent with them.

Steve covered his eyes and started counting out loud very slowly. "One. Two. Three . . ."

When he reached twenty, he opened his eyes and

began his search. Abigail was old enough to be a pretty good hider, but Avery could always be found in plain sight. Right now he was standing behind a floor lamp. Steve, like always, looked around as though he couldn't see his son, then finally moved closer to the lamp. "Where's Avery? Where's Avery?" Steve asked loudly and theatrically. He called to Victoria, "Sweetheart, have you seen Avery?"

"No, honey. I have no idea where he could be!" she called back. Victoria knew her part of the game well.

"I sure do wish I could find him," Steve said.

Behind the floor lamp, Avery giggled.

Steve kept up the ruse of not being able to find Avery until Avery's giggling grew more and more out of control. He finally jumped up and said, "Daddy! I'm here!"

Steve put his hand on his chest and jumped backward as if startled. "There you are! You got me! You're such a good hider!"

"I got you!" Avery said, still overcome with hilarity.

"Now I just need to find your sister," Steve said.

He wandered around the house and didn't see her anywhere. He felt a prickle of anxiety. He knew she was nearby and safe and just playing, but something about her invisibility triggered a primal parental fear. He thought of parents whose children go missing for real, who spend months or years trying to find them. He thought of missing persons reports and kids' faces on milk cartons. He suddenly wanted to find Abigail very badly, to see her beautiful little face.

The bedroom closet. She had hidden there before. He

went into the bedroom but hesitated before opening the closet door. Something inside him didn't want to open it, maybe because it made him think of his night terrors, of the sounds in the house that he investigated with a feeling of dread. Not wanting to know what was causing them, but *needing* to know.

"BOO!" The closet door swung open, and Abigail jumped out.

Steve cried out for real and jumped backward. His heart pounded in his chest. "Wow, you really got me," he said once he had recovered enough to talk.

"Silly Daddy, it was just me," Abigail said. "Did you think it was a ghost?"

"Yeah, I kind of did," Steve said. "You're right. Daddy is very, very silly."

Even in the daylight, even when playing with his kids, the fear was creeping in. He was afraid of noises, sudden movements   even of his own little girl jumping out at him.

He went inside, climbed the ladder, and started back in on the game. It was easy for Steve to create jump scares because he'd just been on the receiving end of one himself. He knew the startled feeling, the cry of shock, the accelerated heartbeat, and then that wash of relief when you realize that it's just a game and you're really safe.

Well, he knew all those things except for the relief. Lately, he never felt like he was safe.

Steve sat in front of the TV, staring at a late-night talk show without really watching it.

Victoria stood in the doorway in her bathrobe and pajamas. "Honey, are you coming to bed?"

"Sure," Steve said, raising the remote to click off the TV. "I thought I might make myself some warm milk first, though. You know, to try to relax."

"You definitely need to relax," Victoria said. "Have some milk, and then maybe I'll give you a shoulder massage."

"That'd be nice," Steve said absently.

Procrastinating going to bed had become a habit with him. It made sense, really. The less time he spent sleeping, the fewer nightmares he'd have.

He drank his warm milk and let Victoria knead his shoulders. Both of these things seemed relaxing at the time he was doing them, but as soon as his head hit the pillow, his body felt like one big ball of tension. It was worse than that. It was terror.

He lay there, his eyes wide open, fighting sleep. Then he heard it. The whirring. The rumbling.

They were inside the walls.

And this wasn't a nightmare because he knew he had never fallen asleep.

Whatever it was that was after him was inside the walls, scurrying, scratching, and looking for a way out. He felt a sudden need to flee the bedroom, but when he stood in the doorway, he heard more rustling and rattling coming from the living room, so they were there, too. He backed up and tried to close the bedroom door, but it was useless. There was no way to lock yourself in and keep intruders out. No one was safe. Steve and his family were sitting ducks, all of them.

A loud bump came from the bedroom wall on Steve's left. He turned to look at it. The surface of the wall began to pulse and throb, forming a large bubble on the surface that reminded Steve of the way cheese bubbles up on a pizza.

Then, with a wet splat, the bubble popped like a zit, and an oily, black substance spattered across the room.

Steve needed to get out of there. He needed to get Victoria out of there. How could she be sleeping through this? He ran over to her side of the bed and shook her shoulder. "Victoria, wake up!"

"What is it? Are the kids okay?" Victoria sat up, rubbing her eyes.

Unable to find words, Steve pointed at the wall, which now had a gaping hole out of which the black slime oozed.

"What?" Victoria said. "Why do you want me to look at the wall?"

"Don't you see it?" Steve said. The black slime was dripping from the hole onto the floor.

Victoria took his hand. "Honey, you're having a nightmare. Lie back down."

"I'm not having a nightmare because I'm not asleep!" Steve yelled. He never raised his voice to his wife or kids, but he was freaking out.

"I know it feels that way because you're walking and talking," Victoria said, "but if you'll lie down and close your eyes, it'll all go away."

Desperate to escape his terror, Steve let himself be coaxed into lying back down. He closed his eyes, feeling how tired he was, how much his body longed for rest. But the noises in the walls didn't stop. There would be no sleep for him tonight.

"This is DJ Dan, the music man," the voice on the radio said. "We've got heavy snow coming on right now! No time to go out and buy milk and bread. Just stay at home and stay safe!"

Abigail looked out the window and announced, "He's right. It's snowing!"

By morning, the yard and surrounding woods were covered in a heavy blanket of snow. The grass and trees looked like they'd been covered in a thick layer of white cake frosting.

At first it was fun. They played board games, made popcorn, and drank hot chocolate. It all felt very cozy.

The trouble was the snow didn't stop. It kept falling, wet and heavy, and the temperature plummeted so it was too frigid for anyone to stay outside for long. Beneath the snow, the roads were a solid sheet of ice. As a result, they were trapped in the house, which was the last place Steve wanted to be.

Because they were there. They were always there even though he only heard them at night. Sometimes (though he would never say it to Victoria because he knew how delusional it sounded) it felt like they had made the snow happen because it put Steve there in the house, right where they wanted him.

The ringing was getting worse, too. The high-pitched sound was always in his head, day and night. Just like the house, he couldn't escape it.

It was day five of the blizzard, and the snowfall was still heavy. Steve, Victoria, and the kids were sitting around the dinner table eating macaroni and cheese and canned green beans Victoria had tried to jazz up with salt, butter, and dill. "I know this meal isn't up to my usual standards of cooking," Victoria said. "But I'm having to dig through the pantry for food since we can't get out to the grocery store."

"I could eat mac and cheese every day," Abigail said. Of the two kids, she was the pickier eater.

"I'm sure you could," Victoria said. "But I bet your daddy would rather have a steak and some salad."

"Actually, I'm kind of digging the mac and cheese," Steve said. It was comfort food, and he certainly needed comfort . . . more than mere food could provide. "Say, when was the last time you checked the weather?"

"Not since this morning," Victoria said. "Unless you count looking out the window."

"Just what we needed," the DJ said in his fake chipper voice. Had somebody turned on the radio? "More snow! The National Weather Service is calling for at least three more inches tomorrow with a high of fifteen degrees. It's gonna be up to our eyeballs, people! This is DJ Dan, the music man, saying stay home and stay safe."

Victoria got up and switched off the radio.

"You know, I've lived in this area all my life, and I've never seen snow like this," Steve said. Back when he was in school, they went whole winters without having any snow days.

"I know. It's like we're at the North Pole," Victoria said.

"Then where's Santa?" Abigail said.

Victoria laughed. "That's an excellent question! If we're stuck in the house, then we deserve presents. Christmas in February!"

Abigail's innocent question made Steve want to cry. Where was Santa indeed? Santa was a symbol of hope, and Steve had lost all hope. Haunted. Hunted. Trapped. And not only trapped but trapped in a dangerous place. Victoria and the kids seemed to think they were safe in the house, but Steve knew better.

He stood up from the table. "I think I'm going to work for a couple more hours."

"Are you sure?" Victoria said. "You've been working all day, and I promised the kids we'd watch a movie together."

"You guys go ahead and get the movie started. I'll be down in a little bit."

Steve knew he was too distracted, too much of a mess, to focus on a movie. Right now the only thing he seemed to be able to focus on was work. He had already completed the first game, so that was one down. Once he submitted all four games, he'd get a big payout from Fazbear Entertainment. Their financial worries would be over, and they could move somewhere else. Somewhere safe where they could be happy together.

Nightmare fuel. He had heard that phrase used to describe a variety of scary images, creepy clowns and dolls, especially. But what Steve was doing was using his nightmares as fuel to power his games. The strange noises and sights, the ongoing feeling of being watched and tracked—he poured all of it into the game. And somehow when he was working, he could almost convince himself that he had control over the forces that terrified him at night. Almost, but not quite. He knew he was spinning out of control, and sometimes he was afraid he had spun so far out he would never find his way back again.

Steve fell into game two and lost track of time. Once he climbed down the ladder, the house was silent. Victoria and the kids were all in bed. Steve decided a hot shower might soothe him—put him in a position to get some sleep. He struggled to remember the last time he had gotten a real night of sleep.

Steve regarded himself in the bathroom mirror. He looked awful. His face was grayish and stubbly. His eyes were bloodshot with dark pouches beneath them. But what scared him most was not the signs of exhaustion but the wildness in his eyes, as if he were a trapped animal.

Who was he kidding? He was a trapped animal.

As he took off his shirt, he felt a small pain in his right forearm. He looked at it and saw a small, shallow cut, the kind of cut one might get from a shaving accident. But that made no sense since he didn't shave his forearms. Examining himself further, he found several small cuts and abrasions on both arms and his chest and belly. He racked his brain trying to figure out where these injuries could have come from. It wasn't like he had a dangerous job; it was pretty hard to hurt yourself sitting in front of a computer all day. The kids had begged him to play Tickle Monster after lunch, and he had obliged, but it wasn't like the kids carried or wore anything sharp or dangerous.

Of course, deep down he knew that the kids weren't the source of his injuries. The source of his wounds was the same as the source of the high-pitched ringing that was inside his head day and night. But as annoying as the ringing was, the cuts and scrapes were worse. They meant that it wasn't just that something wanted to hurt him. Something was hurting him.

Steve stepped into the steaming shower. The hot water stung his cuts and abrasions. If there was an upside to his wounds, it was that they were physical evidence that he wasn't just having night terrors, as Victoria kept insisting. The objects of his terror were real.

Sleep was not an option, so after his shower, Steve sat on the living room couch, not watching TV, not reading, just sitting and waiting for the intruders to make their presence known. For a while, there was nothing, then he saw the glow of the light that came on when someone opened the refrigerator door in the kitchen. There was the slamming of the kitchen cabinet doors. He got up and ran to the kitchen, ready to face whoever or whatever was making the noise.

Avery was standing beside the kitchen sink. Why did the sight of his own son in the dark kitchen make him uneasy?

"Why aren't you in bed, buddy?" Steve asked. He could hear a nervous quaver in his own voice.

"Hi, Daddy. I'm thirsty," Avery said.

"Here, I'll get you a glass of water, but then you have to go back to bed."

"Okay, Daddy."

Steve's hand shook as he held the glass under the faucet. Avery took the glass and sipped from it once, then set it down and toddled back toward his room.

Maybe Steve was having some kind of mental breakdown. The noises he had heard in the kitchen couldn't possibly have been made by a two-year-old child, though, could they? Maybe none of the sounds he was hearing were real. But the cuts and scrapes were real, weren't they?

He went back into the living room and sank to the couch. Outside, the snow made everything silent, and inside, everyone but him seemed to be soundly asleep. It would have been peaceful if he hadn't been so terrified.

Then the noises started—a scrambling and skittering inside the living room walls.

Steve put his hands over his ears. "Stop it, stop it," he begged, rocking back and forth in some primal attempt to comfort himself.

The walls around him pulsated.

A hole appeared in the wall nearest him like a fist had punched through it. But what Steve saw emerging from the hole was not a fist.

It was the head of . . . something.

It was small but bulbous and veined, its large eyes almond-shaped with catlike pupils. It lunged forward from the hole in the wall and parted its jaws to reveal a mouthful of sharp-looking teeth. Its pointed tongue darted out like a snake's when it sniffed the air.

Steve was paralyzed with fear. The only part of him that felt like it was moving was his heart hammering in his chest.

The creature's tongue shot farther out—impossibly far, it seemed—and pierced the skin of Steve's forearm like a hypodermic needle.

The pain was intense. Had the thing poisoned him? He looked at his arm and saw a small red puncture wound with a bruise already forming around it.

Holding his injured arm, he ran from the living room down the hall. The walls in the hallway pulsed, too, and another hole appeared. A green serpentlike head poked out of the hole, its scales a metallic green. It opened its mouth and puked up a large tangle of snakes. The snakes landed on the floor, undulated out of their knot, and slithered around Steve's feet.

Steve hated snakes.

He lifted his feet out of the snake pile and ran to the bedroom. Since the door didn't close or lock properly, he propped a chair up against it.

Victoria sat up in bed. "Steve, what in the world—"

Steve was panting. It was hard to find words. "They're coming out of the walls. Some kind of monsters or aliens or something. And snakes! The hall is full of snakes." He knew how crazy he sounded, but he also knew what he had seen.

"Sit down," Victoria said. "Take deep breaths."

Steve's breathing was fast and shallow. He sat on the bed and tried to slow things down.

"Do you want me to look out in the hall?" Victoria asked.

"No!" Steve yelled louder than he'd meant to. "The snakes! The snakes will get in. I think we're okay with the door closed. I don't think they can get underneath it."

His wife looked at him with a mixture of fear and pity. "I think the stress of developing these games is getting to you, sweetheart. That and the financial pressure and the fact that we've not been able to leave the house for so long. But I promise you, honey, there can't be snakes in the hallway. It's wintertime. The snakes are hibernating."

"The ones in our hallway aren't!" Steve said. "They're wide-awake! Look, I understand that you don't think any of this is real." He started unbuttoning his pajama top. "But look at these! You can't tell me these aren't real." He held out his scratched, cut, and punctured bare arms.

"Oh, my poor darling!" Victoria said, unshed tears sparkling in her eyes. "Just a second. I'll be right back." She disappeared into the bathroom and returned with a tube of antibiotic ointment. She sat next to him on the bed and started dabbing the medicine on his cuts and scrapes. "As soon as the snow melts, we're going to get you some help."

He knew she didn't mean regular medical help. She meant psychiatric help.

She didn't believe him. She was the one person whose

trust he counted on, and she didn't believe him. Steve put his head in his hands. He had lived a lonely life before Victoria and the kids, but somehow he had never felt more alone than he did right now.

"Lie down," Victoria said, gently pushing him back on the bed. "You need to rest."

Steve lay down, but he did not rest. Even though the house was quiet now, the high-pitched ringing in his head was deafening.

In the morning, Steve, head still ringing, opened the bedroom door with a great deal of trepidation, expecting to see the floor squirming with snakes. But the floor looked completely normal, and there was no hole in the wall in the spot where Steve remembered the serpentlike creature poking out its head.

Maybe Victoria was right. Maybe he did need help.

The smells of coffee and bacon were wafting from the kitchen, and Steve was surprised to find the aromas pleasant despite his damaged emotional state. Besides, he had to eat to keep up his strength. He had to work to finish the games. If he finished the games, they'd have the money to leave—if the snowstorm ever stopped.

Victoria was standing at the stove in her bathrobe, simultaneously scrambling eggs and tending to a pan of sizzling bacon. The kids were already at the table with their glasses of orange juice. They were always in such a good mood in the morning. Victoria smiled at him as if everything was normal. "Get us some coffee, why don't ya?" she said.

The radio was on, as it always seemed to be these days, so they could keep track of the weather. After a disconcertingly happy-sounding pop song finished playing, the DJ said, "DJ Dan the music man here, and I've got good news and bad news, folks. The good news is that the chance of precipitation today is just thirty percent, but the bad news is that the temperature won't get above thirty degrees. We might not get any more snow, but the snow we do have isn't going anywhere. So stay inside and stay safe, and I'll keep spinning tunes to keep you happy. And now, by special request, here's the latest hit from Saylor Thrift . . ."

Steve's hand shook as he lifted the pot and poured the coffee into cups. He put milk in Victoria's coffee the way she liked it and sat down with the kids. He tried to act normal, but he knew he was failing.

"What's wrong, Daddy?" Abigail asked.

There you had it. He couldn't act normal enough to fool a four-year-old.

"Nothing, honey," he said. "I'm just tired. I didn't sleep well last night."

"Why?" Avery asked. He was getting into the *why* stage.

Because there are monsters in the walls, Steve thought, but there was no way he was going to say that to a two-year-old. Instead, he said, "I don't know, buddy. Sometimes I just can't sleep."

He ate the bacon and eggs and toast mechanically, the same way he put gas into his car. He needed the fuel to keep going, to do what he had to do, which was finish the games. As soon as he swallowed the last mouthful of food, he chugged the remains of his coffee and got up to go climb the ladder to work.

When he first started working on the games, climbing the ladder into the attic had felt like he was entering the darkness. The horrific world he was creating on the screen as he sat in the windowless attic was a stark contrast to the happiness and light radiated by his wife and children in the rest of the house.

But now the darkness was spilling over into everything.

The only time the high-pitched ringing in his head stopped was when he was working on the game. Or maybe it didn't stop, but the game was the only thing that distracted him from the sound.

The hours fell away as Steve worked. He was on game number three now.

When Victoria called up at him that it was time for lunch, he had been so immersed that he jumped and gasped as though he had been startled by a monster instead of his wife. "Not hungry!" he called back. "Going to work until dinnertime!"

"Okay," Victoria replied. "Let me know if you need anything!"

He didn't answer because he had already fallen back into the game.

Victoria had made spaghetti for dinner again, with garlic bread. Abigail and Avery, their mouths and chins dark orange with sauce, slurped the long noodles and giggled. Victoria was always kind and supportive, and her cooking was always delicious, even now that she was limited to their pantry ingredients because they'd been snowed in for so long. The children were great, too. They were charming and cheerful and never fought like Steve had with his siblings when he was a kid. Steve knew he could have a perfect life with them if they could just get away from this place, this snowbound house of horrors that quite possibly was driving him insane.

But he had the power to get them out, he reminded himself. He was over halfway finished with the game.

"You're quiet tonight," Victoria said.

"Sorry." Steve twirled some spaghetti around his fork. "I'm just having a hard time getting my head out of the game."

"Is it going well?" she asked, reaching over to dab at Avery's orange face with a napkin.

Steve nodded. No matter how unstable and terrified he was in his regular life, somehow his work on the games was really, really good.

"Can we play them when they're ready?" Abigail asked.

"You can play them when you're a little older," Steve said. "Right now they're too scary for you. Sometimes I feel like they're too scary for me, too!"

Abigail and Avery giggled. To them, the idea of a grown-up being scared was so unimaginable that it was funny.

After the kids had bathed and gone to bed, Victoria and Steve cuddled on the couch with the radio playing softly in the background. Even with the volume lowered,

Steve could hear DJ Dan's familiar voice saying, "Even more snow tonight, folks. It looks like we're going to have a white Valentine's Day. If we keep up at this rate, we might have a white Saint Patrick's Day, too!"

Because he was stuck in the house all the time, the dates tended to run together. Steve had forgotten that the next day was Valentine's Day. "I'm so sorry that I've not been able to get you anything for Valentine's Day," Steve said as he stroked Victoria's lustrous hair.

Victoria laughed. "There's no need to apologize. You can't go shopping for cards when you can't get out of the house. The kids are going to make cards out of construction paper tomorrow. Maybe you can make me one, too. Just be neater with the glitter than they are. Cleaning up that stuff is a nightmare."

"You deserve more than a card," Steve said, swept up, as he often was, by Victoria's sheer wonderfulness. It was rare for a person to be equally beautiful on the outside and the inside, but she was. "You deserve red roses and chocolates and a nice piece of jewelry—"

"Shh," Victoria said, putting her index finger gently against his lips. "You're the only Valentine's Day present I need."

"I have no idea how I got so lucky," Steve said.

Victoria smiled. "I feel the same way."

The radio was playing a song that Steve had already heard twice that day. That was always the problem with Top 40 radio; they played the same songs over and over. And to be honest, he was getting a little sick of DJ Dan, too. Didn't that station have any other DJs? DJ Dan seemed to work all hours of the night and day.

Steve stood up and walked over to the window where the radio sat on the sill. "Hey, if you don't mind, I'm going to change the station."

"Oh, don't do that," said Victoria. Her tone sounded casual on the surface, but there was tension underneath.

"Why not?" Steve said. He was already fiddling with the knob. "I'm in the mood for some classic rock, and I'm sure any station we listen to will have updates on the weather." But he couldn't seem to find another station. When he turned it away from the usual pop station, there wasn't even static. Only silence. "Huh, that's weird."

"That's what I was trying to tell you," Victoria said. "It's hard to get a signal out here in the country. For some reason, that pop station's the only one we can get reliably."

"We really are in the middle of nowhere, aren't we?" Steve said, giving up and turning back to the pop station. "No cell phone service, one radio station."

"Yeah," Victoria said, "but I like it. It's peaceful."

Steve had felt anything but peaceful lately. "But don't you ever feel trapped? Especially right now when we've been snowed in so long."

Victoria smiled. "Well, I'd be lying if I said I wouldn't like to be able to go out to the store and maybe grab a pizza somewhere. But overall, I think being snowed in with you and the kids is cozy."

Steve couldn't believe he'd gotten so lucky. Why

would a woman like Victoria even give him the time of day? "Well, there's no one I'd rather be snowed in with than you."

They kissed, and Victoria said, "I think I'm going on to bed. How about you?"

Steve's stomach became a knot of tension at the thought of lying awake in bed and listening to the noises, waiting to see if something burst out of the walls . . . waiting to see if the monsters just wanted to scare him or do him lasting, maybe lethal, harm. "I'll be along in a bit," he said.

"Well, don't stay up all night," Victoria said, getting up from the couch. "Sleep deprivation isn't good for your health—physical or mental."

"I know," Steve said. He was shaky, exhausted, and in a dead panic most of the time. He didn't need to be told his physical and mental health were suffering. "Believe me, I know. I promise I'll try to get some sleep tonight."

Once Victoria was gone, it was like he had lost his safety net and was being plunged into darkness. There was a scraping sound in the walls, like something with sharp claws was inside them. The ringing in his head became so loud it drowned out the music on the radio. He couldn't sit here and be alone. It was so, so much worse when he was alone. The only time he could bear to be alone was when he was working on the game. He was on the last game now; he just had to see it through. He should go to bed. Even though he knew he couldn't sleep, at least Victoria would be there beside him.

As he walked down the hall, the walls pulsated, and the ceiling buckled so it looked like the underside of a hammock. The lowest part of the ceiling cracked, then opened wider, and from the hole emerged a spider the size of a basketball, which dangled just above him from a tendril of web. It was black and hairy, fanged and many eyed. Beside its fangs were pincers, which it rubbed together menacingly.

Steve stood still, afraid to move or even breathe. How could a spider be so big? Was it venomous? If it was, it was probably packing enough venom to kill a herd of elephants.

And then the huge spider's abdomen split open. Out of the opening fell hundreds—maybe thousands—of small spiders like candy falling from a piñata. Steve was covered in spiders. They were in his hair, on his face, and on his hands and arms. They were crawling into his ears, his nose, and his mouth. He screamed and slapped at them with both hands, slapped himself all over, over and over again, in hopes of squishing them.

Victoria came running. "What is it?"

Steve didn't want to talk because he didn't want more spiders to crawl in his mouth, but he managed to say through clenched teeth, "Spiders! They're all over me."

Victoria looked confused and a little alarmed. She took Steve's arm.

"No! Don't touch me! They'll get on you, too."

Victoria drew her hands back in a gesture of surrender. "Okay. But come with me. I need to see you in the light."

Still slapping himself all over, Steve followed her into the bedroom.

She looked him up and down. "Honey, I don't know how to tell you this because I know it's real to you. But I don't see any spiders."

"But how can you not? They're all over—" Steve looked down at his arms, his hands, his shirt. The spiders were gone. He sat down on the edge of the bed. "They were here. They were here." The ringing sound in his head was getting louder and louder, like an ambulance announcing the presence of an emergency. "This place . . . it's making me crazy," he said, on the verge of tears. He stood up. "I have to get out of here. I have to get out of here for a while, even if it's just going for a walk in the snow."

"No," Victoria said. "It's too cold out there, and the snow's too deep. It's not safe."

But Steve was already halfway down the hall. The ringing in his head was growing unbearably loud, like a smoke detector designed to wake up everybody in a burning house.

A smoke detector. That was exactly what it sounded like.

Steve looked at the smoke detector mounted on the ceiling in the living room. Something inside him said, *If you disable the smoke alarm, the sound will stop.* As the ringing in his head continued, he grabbed a poker from the fireplace and hit the smoke alarm with it until he knocked it down on the floor. He continued beating it with the poker, then jumped up and down on it several times for good measure until it was smashed into pieces.

At first there was silence—silence and relief.

But then Steve became aware that although it was finally silent inside his head, he was still surrounded by noise. There was the din of the ever-present DJ Dan on the radio prattling on about the never-ending snowstorm, but there was another sound, too. It was different than what he was used to hearing in the house, though. It wasn't scraping or scuttling but a variety of mechanical sounds—wheels turning, gears grinding. It sounded like he was on the production floor of a small factory.

The sounds weren't the only things that were different. The house looked different, too. The furniture was the same, but there were strange tread marks on the floor. Hinged trapdoors were on the walls and ceiling in the exact places where the creatures had jumped out at him. It was like being inside an amusement park's haunted house with the lights turned on.

He heard more whirring, but whatever was making it was moving toward him from the hallway. He looked around for a hiding place and finally ducked into the coat closet. He tried to pull the closet door shut, but like every other door in this infernal house, it wouldn't close all the way. He ducked behind the hangers of coats and jackets, his heart pounding.

"Honey, where are you?" Victoria's voice called. "You didn't go for a walk in the snow, did you?" Her voice was coming from the living room, but he couldn't hear her footsteps, only a motorized whirring sound.

Steve peeked out from between the coats. Standing in the living room was a robot. It was all steel, with visible wires and circuits. The only part of it that faintly resembled a human being was its face, a mask of plastic with feminine features. "Steve?" Victoria's voice was coming from inside the robot. "Steve? I know you must still be here because your snow boots are beside the door. Where are you, sweetheart?"

Steve's first thought when seeing the robot was *What have you done to Victoria, and why do you have her voice?* But it didn't take long for reality to set in. The robot hadn't done anything to Victoria; the robot was Victoria. Or at least it was what he had been calling Victoria for the past few weeks or months or however long he'd been trapped here.

Steve felt like he might be sick, but he couldn't let himself throw up. If he threw up, he would make a sound, which would ruin his hiding place. He thought of the games of hide-and-seek he had played with the children, full of fun and laughter, so different from the hiding he was doing now.

Wait. The children. The children are in danger from this terrifying thing they thought was their mother. I have to save them.

"Mommy, where's Daddy?" Abigail's voice called.

"Daddy! Daddy!" Avery yelled.

Steve peeked out again from between the coats. What he saw made him shiver, as though the temperature in the room had just dropped forty degrees.

The "children" were robots, too. Smaller ones but also with plastic mask faces with wide robotic eyes and exposed mechanical parts. They moved jerkily around the room, looking behind curtains and under tables, calling, "Daddy? Daddy?"

When Steve didn't respond, the robots stopped using their "human" voices and began to search more aggressively with only the soundtrack of whirring machinery and the pop radio station in the background. The three robots picked up furniture like it was nothing heavier than a pile of sticks. They opened and looked inside the trapdoors even though the spaces were much too small for him to hide in. It was only a matter of time until one of them looked inside the coat closet. What would they do when they found him?

Steve feared for his life.

The pop song on the radio ended, and DJ Dan said, "Stay in and stay safe—well, everybody except you, Steve!"

Steve shook his head as if to jar his brain awake. This was impossible. None of it could be happening.

"Steve, buddy, you need to come out," the familiar voice from the radio said. "Your family is looking for you. Playtime's over, Steve. Victoria, Abigail, Avery . . . they're all getting worried about you. You don't want to worry your beautiful wife and children, do you?"

Through the coats, he watched the animatronic trio go into the kitchen. He knew he couldn't stay in the coat closet forever. If he made it to the bedroom, he could get his car keys. He didn't know how well he'd be able to drive in such deep snow, but it was his only shot so he at least had to try. He ducked out of the coat closet and ran down the hall toward the bedroom, but then he heard the whirring of machinery again and knew they were in the living room. He darted into the bathroom, stepped into the tub, and pulled the shower curtain in front of him. He was out of breath from exertion and terror.

"Steve? Steve, honey?" It was Victoria's voice coming from the hall.

Then he heard the sound of her metal feet on the bathroom tile. The steps grew closer and closer.

In one great sweeping motion, his robot "wife" ripped the shower curtain from the rings holding it in place. Steve was exposed, a sitting duck. He looked at the blank plastic face that was looking at him, and then, with more strength than he knew he possessed, he put both his hands against the robot's cold mechanical shoulders and shoved it as hard as he could.

The force threw the robot off balance, making it fall backward. Steve leaped from the tub, ran past the robot that was already working on righting itself, and made it to the bedroom, shutting the door behind him.

Except the door didn't really shut, and in the hall he could hear the once sweet-sounding, now terrifying voices of his children calling, "Daddy? Da-deeeeee?"

Steve leaned against the door with all his weight. He grabbed the wooden chair from the vanity and angled its back under the doorknob in hopes of making the door harder to open. But the door was the only way out of the room. How long could he hold out?

The three robots were on the other side of the door,

pushing. He was holding them off for now, but he knew he would get tired. They wouldn't.

"Steve? Listen up, Steve." Steve turned his head in the direction of the adult male voice to see the radio that had been in the living room now sitting on the nightstand beside the bed. Had Victoria moved it there in anticipation of Steve ending up in the bedroom? "Steve, this is your buddy DJ Dan the music man," the voice from the radio continued. "I'm here to help you, Steve. You're not going to be able to keep holding that door, buddy. Your arms are already tired, aren't they?"

Steve could feel the muscles in his arms quiver and weaken. He wasn't a spend-hours-at-the-gym kind of guy; he was a sit-hours-at-the-computer guy. He knew his strength was no match for the robots' steel. Still, he tried to hold on.

"Steve?" the voice on the radio continued. "Do you remember when you lived alone in your sad little apartment, working for minimum wage and trying unsuccessfully to get a game off the ground? Do you remember when dinner was a microwaved burrito you ate alone and how sometimes you'd be so lonely you'd go to the bodega and buy something random just so you could make chitchat with the cashier?"

"I remember," Steve said. How did the guy on the radio know so much about him? And why was the guy on the radio talking to him personally anyway? Was all this stuff real, or had he just finally reached his breaking point?

"And now think about how happy you've been since you came here," DJ Dan said in his soothing voice. "No one has ever had a nicer, more beautiful wife than Victoria. And your adorable kids! You always wanted to be a dad, and it's great, isn't it?"

"But it's not real," Steve said. His whole body was pressed against the door, but the robots were standing their ground, pushing from the other side.

"Sure it is, buddy. Everything you felt for your wife and kids—it was as real as it gets. You just have to give yourself permission to be happy."

"But the night terrors—the things in this house—"

"Those weren't real. Those were just there to inspire you while you worked on the game. Say the word, and they're gone. Let go of the door, Steve, and I promise what's on the other side won't come in. You need to stop fighting this and let yourself be happy."

There were tears in Steve's eyes. He had to admit that the moments of joy he had experienced with Victoria and the kids were greater than any other happiness he'd ever known. But the moments of terror he'd experienced in this house were unsurpassed, too. Everything here had been so much more intense than anything that had come before. He felt like all the most important moments in his life had happened here, and yet he had been in this house only a few weeks. "And how do I let myself be happy?" he asked. His voice sounded small, weak.

"It's as easy as pushing a button," DJ Dan's voice said. "If you let go of the door and walk over to the radio, you'll see a red button on its side. If you push that button, you'll have everything you've ever dreamed of. The perfect woman you always wanted, the perfect children you always wanted, and guess what? No more pushing mops or scrubbing toilets for you, buddy, because you'll be one of the world's most successful video game developers! That's a lot of happiness for pushing one little button."

Steve found himself holding the door less forcefully. "But it's not real," he said, even though he felt his resistance weakening.

"Reality is what we make it, Steve," DJ Dan said. "Make your own reality, and make it beautiful. All you have to do is push the button."

Steve thought back to his days of mop pushing and frustration and loneliness. He let go of the door, turned his back on it, and faced the radio.

"You can do it, Steve," DJ Dan's voice urged him. "You can live a life of bliss. Isn't that a beautiful word? *Bliss*."

Steve moved closer to the radio. He heard a creak as the bedroom door opened behind him.

There was the red button. All he had to do was push, and the fantasy would become reality. It was such a beautiful fantasy. And what favors had reality ever done for him? Steve's hand shook as he reached out toward the radio.

He pushed the button.

The high-pitched ringing filled Steve's head, filled the room, and seemed to fill the whole world. Steve clapped his hands over his ears, but it did nothing to muffle the horrible cacophony. He fell to his knees as the room started to spin.

And then, just as suddenly, everything was still. Steve used the nightstand to steady himself as he rose to his feet. He looked around the bedroom. Everything looked normal.

And then he saw her.

Victoria was standing in the doorway. Her blue-black hair was like a halo around her lovely face. She was wearing the same green dress she wore the first time they met. His favorite dress. He could say she was just as beautiful as the day they met, but that would be a lie. She was even more beautiful.

"Victoria." He breathed her name in a reverent whisper.

"Sweetheart," she said, looking at him with love in her green-flecked brown eyes. She opened her arms to him.

This time, Steve didn't hesitate.

He went to her. He wrapped his arms around her and pressed his lips to hers.

Bliss. That was the perfect word for what he was feeling. His bliss was so great that he barely felt the continuous stabbing in the vicinity of his heart.

HAPPS

AIDEN FLUNG OPEN THE DOOR IN FRONT OF HIM AND STOMPED OUT INTO THE CHAOS THAT WAS THE MAIN CONCOURSE THROUGH THE FREDDY FAZBEAR'S MEGA PIZZAPLEX. THE DOOR HIT THE WALL WITH A BANG LOUD ENOUGH TO GET THE ATTENTION OF A GROUP OF GIGGLING GIRLS PASSING BY THE EXIT AREA OF THE LASER TAG ARENA. AIDEN RECOGNIZED THE GIRLS IMMEDIATELY; THEY WERE SENIORS AT HIS SCHOOL.

The door rebounded and hit Aiden from behind. The girls laughed at him.

One of the girls, a cute redhead, Nora, raised her brows and pointed when she saw Aiden's swollen left eye. "Nice shiner, Aiden." She put emphasis on the second syllable in his name and changed the *e* to an *o*, pronouncing his name Ai*don*, instead of the way it was supposed to be pronounced—with more inflection on the *Ai* and an *e* sound instead of an *o* in the second syllable.

This mangling of Aiden's name was pretty universal at his school. It had started when Aiden, new to the school, had a wild idea and tried out for a talent competition.

Unnaturally tall and skinny for his fifteen years, Aiden was burdened with wild bushy hair, a beaky nose, no chin, and lopsided eyes. He knew he was nothing to look at so he tried to make up for it with unusual abilities and knowledge. Aiden was an accomplished juggler. He had mad skills with a Hula-Hoop and a jump rope, and could do things with a yo-yo that no one else had thought of. He'd convinced himself it would be a good way to meet people and fit in if he put together a routine showcasing these gifts and presented them in his new school's talent show. His plan, unfortunately, had backfired. In front of the dozens of kids hanging out to watch the auditions, Aiden was called onto the stage by clueless Mrs. Marchant, the head of the theater department.

"Ai*don*," she had warbled when he'd come onstage with his jump rope, Hula-Hoop, juggling pins, and yo-yo.

Everyone probably would have forgotten the incident if he hadn't completely bungled his routine. Aiden had an arsenal of tricks, but they all failed him that day. Self-conscious, he had ended up getting so entangled with his rope and his yo-yo that he'd fallen down and then managed to trip off the stage.

Story of his life.

"Ignore them," Aiden's one and only friend, Jace, said now. "The black eye makes you look tough."

Aiden snorted. He kicked at one of the neon squares on the floor of the walkway through the Pizzaplex. "Yeah, right. Wait until Landon tells everyone how I got it. Jackass. Laser tag is supposed to be about shooting the laser guns, not hand-to-hand combat. He threw that elbow on purpose."

Jace sighed and pulled Aiden, oblivious of his surroundings, out of the path of a group of kids chasing one another through the Pizzaplex. "Yeah, he probably did. News flash: he's a jerk."

Aiden, steaming, stalked away from the laser tag arena. Bumping into people right and left, he barely heard or saw anything around him. He was vaguely aware that Jace was trotting after him, but the bright lights and cheerful sounds of the Pizzaplex were being muted by the buzz of Aiden's rage.

He was so *tired* of being treated like crap, like he was a ball trapped inside a pinball machine, being slapped this way and that by his classmates and his parents. He was tired of being a pawn. He wanted some *control*.

"Aiden." Jace tugged at Aiden's shirt sleeve. When Aiden ignored him, he tugged harder. "Aiden!"

Aiden stopped and whirled on his friend. "What?!"

Jace's face tightened, and he hunched his shoulders. Already small for a ninth grader, Jace could practically curl into a ball when he felt rejected or criticized. Unlike Aiden, Jace wasn't bad-looking. He had a normal face and perfectly normal black hair, but he was too cute—as in little-kid cute. He was too small and too fragile, and he had an unfortunate little-boy voice to go with his looks. This shoved him out into the same no-man's-land of unpopularity that Aiden had lived in ever since he was five years old. The day before his first day in kindergarten, Aiden had overheard his mom telling a friend that she wished his "sweet" personality would overcome his "unfortunate homeliness." Her hopes had been, well, hopeless.

Aiden immediately felt bad when he looked at Jace's crushed expression. Jace was the only person who treated Aiden like he mattered. "Sorry, Jace. I'm just pissed, is all."

Jace nodded. "I get it. I'm sorry Landon elbowed you. I should've found a way to have your back. But he kind of outweighs me. Plus, besides the laser gun, all I have is this." Jace pulled out the Swiss Army knife his mom had given him for his birthday. He was ridiculously happy with the gift, as if the tiny knife and its itsy-bitsy scissors and corkscrew and file and screwdriver could transform little Jace into an invincible warrior.

Aiden punched Jace's shoulder lightly. "Well, next time, pull that thing out and run him through."

Jace laughed. He pretended to wield the knife like a sword.

A little girl in braided pigtails bounced off Aiden's legs, and he felt something wet and sticky on his skin. He looked down just in time to see the little girl's huge smiley-face sucker finish swiping his forearm.

"Ew!" Aiden yanked his arm back and glared at the little girl; she didn't even notice him.

Jace plucked at Aiden's sleeve again. This time, Aiden didn't snap. He let Jace pull him out of the flow of the crowd, back against a bright striped wall next to the neon-lit entrance to the bumper car arena. Aiden glowered at Freddy's themed cars. Normally, he liked bumper cars; they were a great way to let off steam. Today, though, somehow the shiny little shoe-shaped pods painted to look like Freddy's animatronic characters were just too perky.

"What do you want to do now?" Jace asked.

Aiden pulled his gaze from the chaos of the zigzagging, careening bumper cars. Listening to the cars' buzzing and the kids' whooping, he shrugged.

So far today, he and Jace had played their favorite arcade games, spent some time in the VR booths, ridden the roller coaster, and stuffed themselves with pizza. None of that had done it for Aiden. He just wasn't in the mood to have fun today. He'd been ready to give up and go home and watch TV when Jace had suggested laser tag. Aiden had agreed when he'd seen Landon and his friends go into the arena. Aiden hated Landon, and the idea of shooting the smug jerk with a laser gun had sounded like a good idea.

Aiden gingerly touched his still-swelling eye. He grimaced. So much for that good idea.

"Why don't we go tubing?" Jace asked. "Remember how much fun it was last time? When we scared those little kids?"

Despite his mood, Aiden smiled. "Yeah, that was pretty cool."

Tubing was Jace and Aiden's word for clambering through Freddy's Fortress, a massive maze of climbing and sliding plastic pipes that—entwined with Fast Freddy, the Pizzaplex's superfast roller coaster—embraced the entire circumference of the center. They'd only recently checked out the maze because it was advertised more toward the younger kids than toward teens; they'd originally gone poking around the maze because they'd been avoiding some bullies who had been hassling them in the arcade.

"At least you shouldn't get hurt in the tubes," Jace said, panting. "Happs won't let that happen!" He laughed his patented girlish twitter.

Aiden grinned. "Good old Happs."

Happs, Aiden and Jace had discovered when they'd first explored the maze, was a maintenance and safety bot designed to prevent injuries in the maze. H.A.P.P.S. stood for Helpful Automated Pipe Protection Server; it was a robot that roamed the tubes—or pipes, checking to be sure everything was in good order and helping out kids who had fallen or were lost.

Aiden and Jace got a big kick out of Happs. They thought the robot's huge lit-up smile and large foam hands were hilarious. When they'd first encountered him, they'd wanted to adopt him. *Wouldn't it be great if we had a Happs to clear the way for us at school?* Jace had asked as they'd left the maze after the first time they'd explored it.

Aiden had warmed to the idea. "Yeah. Happs could just toss aside all the jerks."

Jace laughed. "And do our homework for us."

"And clean our rooms."

"He could do all our chores!"

Aiden chuckled. "That would be cool."

"And lock my dad out of the house when he gets in his bad moods," Jace said.

This last thought had sobered them. Aiden's parents didn't approve of him; they tended to ignore him. But Jace's dad was mean. There was nothing funny about that.

Now Aiden slung an arm around his friend's shoulders. "Yeah, let's go tubing."

Jace grinned, and the two boys stepped into the flow of the crowd rushing from one part of the Pizzaplex to the other. As soon as they did, Aiden felt the pulsing heat in his temples begin to abate. He mentally shook off the image of Landon's perpetual *I'm-better-than-you* smirk.

The entrance to Freddy's Fortress was on the opposite side of the Pizzaplex from the bumper cars. It would take several minutes to get there at Jace's pace . . . his small legs couldn't stride as fast as Aiden's could.

When Aiden and Jace had come to the Pizzaplex the first time, the place had been overwhelming. It was huge! Fortunately, though, its layout was pretty simple. The Pizzaplex was shaped like a pizza, under a massive neon-lit dome topped by a backlit pizza-themed stained-glass cupola. Because of this round configuration, Jace had told Aiden he thought the Pizzaplex was sort of a giant clock of fun. Because Freddy's Pizzeria was the inspiration for everything in the Pizzaplex, Jace suggested that the big dining area where the pizza was served was noon on the clock. Every other main part of the Pizzaplex was another hour on the clock face. Laser tag was at 4:00, the entrance to Freddy's Fortress was between the carnival games area in the 2:00 position, and the arcade was in the 3:00 position. Unfortunately, when Aiden had charged out of the laser tag arena, he'd headed left instead of right. So, they'd ended up in front of the bumper cars, which was at 7:00 on Jace's imaginary Pizzaplex clock face.

It didn't take long to hurry past the Role Play area, something Aiden and Jace hadn't tried yet, and the employees-only section of the Pizzaplex—the behind-the-scenes janitorial, storage, maintenance, kitchen, and security areas. After that, they strode past the shopping area and then on by the packed dining area and its enticing aroma of pepperoni and onions. Even though Aiden and Jace had filled up on pizza already, the food still smelled good.

As they moved through the crowd, go-carts shot past on the track that ran parallel to the walkways and sometimes dipped under pedestrian bridges. The Doppler hum of the carts' electric motors was like a bass line to the crowd noise.

Just beyond the dining room, the carousel spun in kaleidoscopic color and tinkling musical sound as they passed it. And just after that, the carnival games area bulged in chaotic crowds of laughing people shouting encouragement as they tried to win plush Freddy's character prizes.

Finally, Aiden and Jace made it to the entrance to Freddy's Fortress. They got in line behind two dark-haired little girls who were dancing happily to the music blasting through the Pizzaplex's sound system.

With a neon arch like all the other Pizzaplex venue openings, the entrance to Freddy's Fortress was long, narrow, and disorienting. Painted in a black-and-white pinwheel illusion pattern, the entrance made you feel like you were stepping into infinity. You felt like you were leaving the real world behind, being lured into a topsy-turvy realm that would trap you forever. Aiden and Jace thought it was supercool.

"Maybe we should paint the inside of our fort like this when we build it this summer," Jace said now.

Aiden thought about it. "Think we could pull it off? I don't know how to paint illusions."

"I don't, either," Jace said, "but we could figure it out. Right? We're our own universe, aren't we? We can make whatever we want."

Aiden grinned at his friend. He gave Jace a high five. Jace returned it.

Jace and Aiden had been friends for only a few months, since Aiden's dad had been transferred to the town and Aiden had started at the new school—in the middle of the term. Aiden hated starting schools in midterm. Why couldn't his dad stick with one job in one town?

Even though Aiden hadn't known Jace long, he was closer to Jace than he'd ever gotten to his friends in previous towns. Aiden was a one-friend-at-a-time guy—not by choice; it just seemed to work out that way.

Jace had been the only kid who hadn't decided that Aiden's jump-roping, Hula-Hooping, juggling, yo-yoing fiasco left him unqualified for friendship. Jace had come to sit with Aiden at lunch the day Aiden had so spectacularly made a fool of himself.

"Come to laugh at the new class clown?" Aiden had asked Jace when he'd sat down and opened his brown bag.

"Nope. Came to meet the bravest guy in the school," Jace said, pulling out an array of plastic containers that Aiden would later find out contained a sun-dried tomato and crab salad sandwich on sourdough bread, wild greens in raspberry vinaigrette, and a kiwi fruit tart. Jace had sophisticated food tastes. The only food he and Aiden agreed on was pizza—and Jace always wanted his with weird toppings like artichoke hearts and goat cheese and caramelized onions. They always got a half-and-half pizza—Aiden was a plain pepperoni guy.

After Jace had pulled out his fancy lunch, he'd grinned and offered a hand. "It took guts to do what you did."

Aiden had stared at Jace's elfish face. "You're not messing with me, are you?"

Jace shook his head. "I don't know how to mess with people. I'm just, well . . . me, I guess. Not that too many people appreciate that. But it is what it is. I'm my own universe."

Aiden laughed. He liked that. "Well, do you have room in that universe for a plus one?" he asked.

Jace had nodded. The two had shaken hands, and that was that. They'd been friends ever since.

It hadn't mattered after that bonding moment that

Aiden and Jace didn't have a lot in common. Jace didn't care that Aiden dressed like a slob—in baggy jeans and faded T-shirts and dirty, scuffed boots, and Aiden didn't care that Jace dressed like a little adult—in pressed khaki slacks and button-down shirts and old-fashioned sneakers. It didn't matter that Jace was more interested in art and music than academics and that Aiden loved learning things and got straight As (something that contributed to his classmates' disdain—what was wrong with being smart?). It wasn't a problem that Jace was obsessed with reading novels and collecting old clocks and that Aiden was obsessed with his ropes and pins and hoops and yo-yos. They always found plenty to talk about because Aiden liked to hear about what Jace was doing and Jace liked to hear about what Aiden was doing.

They did have some common ground—they both liked to watch old movies and shows on TV and they both liked to play games. And they both loved Freddy's. They'd been thrilled when Freddy Fazbear's Mega Pizzaplex had opened up.

Fortunately, only a few kids were lined up to get into Freddy's Fortress. Aiden and Jace waited just a couple minutes before they were crawling into the first shiny red tube that led into the heart of the maze.

Although the tubes that made up the climbing maze might have been designed for the smaller kids, they were large enough for adults to crawl through. About four feet in diameter, the rounded tunnels had plenty of space for even Aiden's tall, gangly frame.

Aiden and Jace crawled quickly when they entered the

maze, and it didn't take much time for them to reach the end of the first tube, which was only about twenty feet long. At the end of that twenty feet, the maze branched out in several directions. Some of the offshoots had ladders attached to the tubing—Aiden thought of these as ladder pipes; they angled up from one level to another like stairs. Some of the tunnels had even sharper angles of ascent; these were studded with big hand- and footholds like the kind on climbing walls—Aiden thought of these as climbing pipes. Some tubes climbed more gradually than either the ladder pipes or the climbing pipes, so neither ladder rungs nor hand- and footholds were needed. Some of the tubes were level, leading into far off areas of the maze before heading upward. And some of the tubes were slides. Aiden and Jace liked those the best.

Listening to Jace puff along behind him, Aiden pointed to one of the level tunnels. "Let's go this way," he said. He wanted to get deep into the labyrinth of the fortress, as far away from life as possible.

"I'm right behind you," Jace said unnecessarily.

Aiden led the way into what was now a bright orange tunnel. Although the tunnels were formed of transparent plastic that allowed you to see through them, the plastic was tinted in a variety of bright colors, some solid-colored and some multicolored in mind-blowing patterns like stripes or polka dots or illusions similar to the pinwheel shapes at the entrance. A few tunnels were just plain clear plastic. Some were so black they were nearly opaque.

At first, Aiden and Jace had hypothesized that the colors and patterns were designations to help navigate the maze, but after exploring the fortress for hours, they hadn't discerned any logical order to the colors. The various shades seemed to be as random as the twists and turns, rises, and drops in the fortress.

In addition to the many-hued passageways in the maze, the fortress contained intriguing, ever-shifting mirrored partitions. These partitions seemed to show up suddenly and randomly. A tunnel could be wide open one minute, and a couple minutes later, it was blocked with one of the mirrors.

These mirrors fascinated Aiden and Jace. The first time they'd encountered one blocking a section that had been open when they'd passed it just moments before, they'd started trying to figure out the timing and location of the mirrors.

They assumed the mirrors showed up to further confuse the already bewildering layout of the maze. They definitely had that effect. One afternoon the previous week, it had taken Aiden and Jace over an hour to find their way around one such suddenly appearing mirror so they could make their way back out of the maze.

Now Aiden led Jace past one of the mirrors. He paused at a junction of another tunnel leading to the left and a climbing pipe heading up and to the right. "Which way?" he asked Jace. "Your turn to choose."

Jace wriggled up next to Aiden and assessed his options. He looked to both sides and straight ahead.

Because the pipes in the fortress were transparent, they could see into other pipes around them. To their left, a couple of little girls were crawling around a bend leading away from where Aiden and Jace crouched. To the right, a couple tubes over, a tousle-headed toddler was being towed along by a clearly exasperated older girl; she was probably the little kid's sister.

Jace pointed at a ladder tube. "Let's go up. Maybe we'll find one of those long twisty slides. I like those."

Aiden grinned. He liked the twisty slides, too. They started at the top of the three-story-high fortress, and they ended up on the venue level of the Pizzaplex. Because they wound around in a tight spiral, the ride down was long and fun. Unfortunately, though, to get to the top of a slide, you had to figure out the way to the correct climbing pipes to get to the top of the fortress. Aiden and Jace had only found the top of the curlicue slides three times. Maybe they'd get lucky today.

"You lead," Aiden told Jace.

Jace nodded and reached for the closest bright purple handhold on the blue-and-pink swirl-patterned climbing pipe walls. Aiden waited for Jace to work his way up the tube a few feet before Aiden started following his friend. He took a deep breath, inhaling the familiar smell of the maze.

The pipes in the fortress had a sort of chemical odor— Aiden figured it was the plastic. In addition to that sharp smell, the pipes sometimes smelled like sweat or dirty socks. Layered over those smells was the scent of the disinfectant spray that Happs applied liberally as he made his way through the maze.

Skirting around a wad of chewing gum, Aiden thought about Happs. He and Jace had discussed the robot a lot.

They had concluded Happs was a programming marvel. Not only was Happs designed to get kids out of trouble in the maze, he was also a janitorial and maintenance bot. His technology apparently was cutting edge. Aiden had read up on it after they'd encountered him their first time in the maze.

According to the articles Aiden had found, Freddy's Fortress had been the subject of heated debate when it was first proposed. Smaller versions of the climbing and sliding tubes had been tried in other famous kid-focused pizza places, and they'd been a big disaster. The problem wasn't just safety. Yes, little kids sometimes got stuck or hurt themselves when they fell. Once, Aiden read, a fire-and-rescue team had to be called in to extricate a teen who'd been a little too big to round a corner in one of the pipes.

Stuck kids, however, weren't the real issue with climbing pipes. The real drawback to the installations was sanitation.

When they were first built in the other pizza places, employees were sent into the pipes several times a day to try to keep them clean. This job, however, was too big and too unpleasant for a minimum-wage employee to do well. Hygiene became a big concern. Many parents refused to let their kids go in the tubes; something that led to frequent noisy public tantrums. Some of the restaurant managers had the climbing pipes removed. The pipe mazes were nearly phased out of the other restaurant chains, but eventually larger pipes were built (to prevent stuck teens), and better cleaning procedures were put into place.

Proponents of Freddy's Fortress had pointed to the relative success of the other chains' newest pipe mazes to argue for the inclusion of the fortress in the Pizzaplex. Opponents to Freddy's Fortress had argued that the massive size of the fortress maze would multiply safety and cleaning issues exponentially. The idea was nearly scrapped until the tech geniuses at Fazbear Entertainment came up with Happs. They programmed Happs to be so efficient and autonomous that no human employee ever had to go in the fortress. Happs kept the entire network of pipes sparkling clean and hygienic and in good repair, and he made sure no big jerks got stuck.

At the top of their climb, Jace paused to catch his breath. As Jace wiped his face, Aiden waited patiently.

The climbing holds in the tubes were placed close together so even the smallest kids could use them. And the angles of ascent in the tubes weren't extreme. It wasn't hard to work your way up through the fortress. Jace, however, wasn't in the best shape. Given that his only physical activities were picking up a book or tinkering with the clocks he liked to collect, he got out of breath pretty easily.

"We have four choices here," Jace said finally. "I don't see any sign of a slide."

Aiden glanced down the lateral tunnels extending out from their current location. Nope. No slides.

To the left, though, down one of the angled tunnels, Aiden could see three little kids.

Aiden pointed. "Let's go see if we can scare some munchkins."

Jace laughed. "Good idea." He crawled into the tunnel Aiden had indicated. Aiden followed.

The new tunnel twisted sharply three times before winding around to a pipe that intersected with the one the little kids were in. Jace paused at the entrance to the intersecting pipe.

Assuming a soldier-like demeanor, Jace made a series of convoluted hand motions designed to mimic those he and Aiden had seen in action movies. First, Jace pointed at his eyes, then at Aiden's eyes, and then at the little kids, who were crawling happily, completely oblivious of their watchers.

Jace made a circular gesture at the intersection pipe. Then he made a sort of crawling motion with his fingers. He used his other hand to make a larger crawling motion before dropping his second hand onto his first hand, apparently indicating a surprise ambush.

Aiden laughed. Jace immediately put a finger to his lips and gave Aiden a mock-stern look. Aiden stifled his laughter and pretended to zip his lips.

Of course, all this pantomime was ridiculously unnecessary. Even if they'd laughed uproariously and even yelled their lungs out, the little kids would have barely heard them.

The pipes in Freddy's Fortress were surprisingly well sound insulated. Aiden had read up on that, too. Apparently, the plastic used to form all the pipes in the maze wasn't ordinary plastic. Some kind of special polymer had been included in the mix to soundproof the tubes. They weren't *completely* soundproof, obviously, but they muted sound enough that between the plastic and the loud music and crowd noise filling the Pizzaplex, sound didn't carry far in the maze.

Jace made a *with-me* motion, and he crawled into the intersecting pipe. Aiden followed.

They crawled about thirty feet or so before Jace came to a stop and held up a fist. Aiden grinned and obediently stopped, too. Jace pointed to his right.

They were close enough to the little kids now that they could hear them. There were three of them, two boys and a girl. The girl seemed to be the one in charge of the little group. She sounded really bossy.

"We need to go up here first, Bobby. This is the right way," she said in a mom-like tone.

"But I want to go down the slide," Bobby whined.

"Yeah, me too," the second boy said.

"You're both stupid," the bossy girl said.

Jace looked over his shoulder at Aiden. He mimed sticking a finger down his throat. Aiden understood. Jace had a bossy older sister. He probably sympathized with Bobby and the other boy.

Jace held up a finger. Then two fingers.

Aiden positioned himself to follow Jace's lead.

Jace held up a third finger. Then he pointed.

Jace and Aiden let out bloodcurdling screams and crawled furiously around the bend. They crowded in next to each other. With faces contorted into monster-like expressions, they reached out as if to grab the little kids.

All three kids—who looked to be maybe five or

six—screamed. One of the boys, a small kid with straggly brown hair, screamed louder than the others. The other boy, round-faced and dark-skinned, didn't just scream— he turned to scurry away. The girl, a cute blonde with bright blue eyes, stopped screaming almost as quickly as she started. She instantly figured out that Aiden and Jace were messing with her and her friends. She had been startled into screaming, but she wasn't scared of them.

Sitting back on her heels, the girl put her hands on her hips. Wearing red pants, a black shirt, and a red-and-black-striped headband, the little girl looked like a pint-size fierce warrior. All she needed was face paint to complete her look.

The girl glared at Aiden and Jace. "You're mean!" she said.

Aiden lunged forward and roared at her.

It was a good roar, but it didn't bother the girl at all. Instead of reacting to Aiden, she elbowed the boy next to her. He was still screaming. "Shut up, Bobby. It's just a couple big stupid boys being jerks."

Bobby, who had screwed up his eyes, his face bright red, opened his eyes. He stopped screaming.

The girl turned and looked at the retreating boy. "Get back here, Arlo. Stop being a scaredy-cat."

Aiden looked at Jace, who was staring at the girl with a wide-eyed frown. He looked like he couldn't decide whether to be surprised by the girl's nonchalance or annoyed by it.

The girl turned back to Aiden and Jace. "You're stupid," she announced. *Stupid* seemed to be her favorite word.

Suddenly, Aiden *felt* pretty stupid. Why did he and Jace think it was so much fun to torment little kids?

"You're bullies, too," the little girl said. She started crawling toward them. "Now get out of the way. Or I'll punch you."

Aiden didn't doubt the girl would follow through with her threat. He nudged Jace, and the two teens turned to crawl away into another pipe.

They weren't running away or anything, obviously. Who ran from a five-year-old? Aiden's ego wanted him to be clear on that as he and Jace crawled.

So why did they retreat so quickly? Well, for sure, it wasn't that Aiden was afraid of a five-year-old girl's punch. The real reason he wanted to get away from the girl as fast as possible was that he didn't think his ego could survive being bested by the munchkin he'd been trying to scare. Served them right, he figured. Scaring little kids wasn't exactly a nice thing to do.

"Yeah, that's right!" the little girl called out behind them. "Run away! And don't come back!"

Aiden didn't bother responding to the little powerhouse. He was ashamed of himself.

Apparently, Jace wasn't feeling too good about himself, either. He didn't say anything for several minutes as Aiden led them through a series of several twisting tubes. Finally, at a junction with three new pipe offshoots, Aiden stopped and looked back at Jace.

"Do you feel like as big a jerk as I do?" he asked his friend.

Jace dropped his head. "Yeah."

They sat in silence for a few seconds. Aiden gazed past Jace to watch little kids in other pipes. Then he craned his neck to look down onto the main walkway of the Pizzaplex. He suddenly wished he and Jace were down there having fun instead of being up here trying to take out their frustrations on poor little kids—not that the little girl had fit that description at all.

Jace nudged Aiden. "Let's find a slide and then get out of here."

"Good idea. You lead."

Jace nodded. He crawled into the nearest pipe opening. Aiden went in behind him.

A few feet along the new pipe, Jace started to lead them past a pink offshoot tube to the right. Suddenly, he gasped and faltered.

"What?" Aiden asked. He squeezed up next to his friend to look down the pink tube.

Jace laughed sheepishly. "It's just Happs. He surprised me, is all."

Aiden didn't tease Jace for his reaction. Aiden could see how Happs had startled Jace.

The robot was only a couple feet away. Facing a green tube that led off from the pink tube, Happs's big foam hands were pressed against the heavy plastic on either side of the green tube's opening. Aiden could see that beyond the hole, the tube's green plastic was bulging abnormally.

Apparently sensing Aiden and Jace watching him, Happs rotated his squarish head and smiled widely.

"Hey, Happs," Jace said.

"Hello," Happs said in a chirpy tone. Happs's voice

was robotic and stiff, but it was pitched high and came out in a cheerful singsong cadence. "I'm Happs. Are you lost?"

From what Aiden and Jace had discovered in their previous encounters with Happs, this was Happs's go-to first line.

"No, we're fine, Happs," Aiden said.

"I am happy that you are fine," Happs replied.

Conversation wasn't Happs's forte. He was a pretty quiet robot. Besides his few simple phrases, the only sounds Happs emitted were the hums and whirs of his servos and the churning of the black rubber treads that he used to get around. The treads took the place of legs and feet. In spite of Happs's stiff speech, he was likable. The robot was clearly designed to make kids feel safe.

About two and a half feet tall, Happs appeared to be made of a combination of plastic, metal, rubber, and foam. Happs's torso was shaped like an isosceles quadrangle (a fact Aiden was proud to know—he liked geometry), and it was made of gray metal. A couple small doors were inset in the torso. Aiden wasn't sure what they were for. Articulated metal arms—gray except for black-and-yellow security stripes painted on the biceps area—extended from the quadrangle's sides. The arms ended in big white foam hands that looked like the WE'RE #1 foam hands that kids wore at football games. A round plastic head sat on the short edge of the quadrangle-shaped torso; the head was topped with a flashing yellow security light.

Although Happs's big rubber treads and gray metal

gave him a vaguely tanklike appearance, his face countered that with an industrial look. Featuring bright yellow eyes, round "cheeks" of more black-and-yellow-striped paint, and a large tilted mouth full of backlit grinning teeth, Happs had a friendly demeanor.

As Aiden and Jace looked on, Happs lifted one of his big foam hands and gave the teens a thumbs-up. Aiden and Jace returned the gesture. As soon as they did, Happs turned back to the opening of the green tube in front of him.

Something clicked, and a swishing sound accompanied the sudden appearance of a mirror. The mirror slid into place like a spaceship door, blocking the green tube. As soon as the mirror partition settled, Happs turned and trundled on down the offshoot, away from Aiden and Jace. As he went, one of the little doors on Happs's torso opened, and a third "arm" unfolded from the opening. On a telescoping extender, the arm ended in a curved sponge that wiped the pipe's interior as Happs passed through it. The arm moved so fast it was hard to follow it. Not only was the arm sponging, it was also spraying the floral-smelling disinfectant that Happs used liberally. The sponging and spraying made Happs look a little like a miniature mobile car wash.

"That was cool!" Jace said.

Aiden pulled his gaze from Happs. He nodded and crawled past Jace into the pink tube. He poked at the mirror that had just appeared. "There has to be some mechanism here." He ran his fingers along the edge of the mirror.

Jace crawled up next to him, and he, too, prodded the edges of the mirror. "I don't think Happs is a wizard, so yeah, you're right—the mirror didn't come out of nothing."

The boys explored the edges of the mirror for another minute or so. They found nothing.

Aiden plopped back on his butt, crossing his legs. "I think I know why these mirrors show up."

"Why?"

"Before this mirror blocked the opening, I saw what looked like a problem with the tube. I wonder if they use the mirrors as barriers to shut off parts of the maze that need maintenance, kind of like emergency doors that close in a submarine if it starts to take on water."

Jace nodded. "That makes more sense than using them to confuse us. And for sure they'd have some way of handling problems. They wouldn't want to have to shut down the whole fortress if there's an issue in one area."

Aiden gave the mirror one last look, then nudged Jace. "Come on. Let's stop hassling little kids. Let's see if we can find Happs again. Maybe he'll lead us somewhere interesting." Aiden pointed down the pink tube.

Happs was no longer in sight because the pink corridor took several sharp turns, and another tube bisected it—that tube obscured the view of the pink pipe behind the turns. But Happs couldn't have gotten too far. From what Aiden had seen, Happs's rubber treads didn't appear to be built for speed.

"Sure. Why not?" Jace agreed. "You lead now."

Aiden nodded and started crawling down the pink

tube. He led Jace around the bends, then paused when he encountered six different options. Because they were at the top of the maze, none of the tubes let upward. Three were lateral, and three headed downward. Two of those three had gradual descents meant for more crawling. One of the three was a slide; a bright blue see-though pipe canted in a sharp descent.

"Hey," Jace said, panting as he reached Aiden's side. "You found a slide!"

Aiden nodded. He looked at the other tube openings. He was conflicted. He wanted to find Happs again, but the slides were fun.

"I know what you're thinking," Jace said. "We were going to look for Happs. But what if he went down the slide, too?"

"That's a good point." Aiden turned toward the slide opening. "Let's go for it."

Aiden flipped onto his butt so he could wriggle into the slide feetfirst. He listened to Jace slither into place behind him.

"Hang on to my belt loop," Aiden said.

"Don't worry. I will!" Jace replied. "I haven't forgotten."

Jace was talking about the second time they'd found a curling slide. About halfway down, they'd gotten split up when the slide forked and sent them in opposite directions. Fortunately, they'd both managed to find their way to the maze's exit pretty quickly, and they'd reentered the maze together. The next time they'd used a slide, they'd made sure they were hooked together so they ended up in the same place.

"Ready?" Aiden asked.

"Ready."

Aiden pushed off the slide walls, and he and Jace whooped as they shot downward, whipping around a sharp curve. Skimming through the fluorescent-blue pipe, Aiden felt cool air on his face, and for an instant, he felt free. If only he could get the instant to last forever.

Even though Aiden kept busy with his hooping and juggling and yo-yoing and jump-roping and he got great grades, he wasn't exactly happy. The truth was, Aiden pretty much hated his life. He often wished he could have a do-over. He knew he couldn't change his looks, but maybe if he hadn't tried to compensate for them by learning weird skills, other kids would have taken him more seriously. Maybe his parents would've paid more attention to him. Maybe . . .

Aiden shot out of the blue pipe and landed in a dimly lit pit filled with glow-in-the-dark rubber balls. Jace tumbled over Aiden, then popped upright. The two swam through the balls toward a neon-marked opening on the far side of the pit. As soon as they were out of the pit, they crawled into a yellow-and-purple-striped pipe. It was one of three options, and they picked it randomly.

"That was a good one!" Jace panted as they crawled.

"Yeah," Aiden agreed. He stopped at a junction with another pipe. He gestured at it. "You want to go that way, or do you want to keep going straight?"

Jace looked at the nearly opaque pipe that led to the left. He pointed down the yellow-and-purple one. "Let's keep going. I don't like the really dark tubes."

Aiden nodded. "Yeah, I'm with you on that." Aiden continued leading the way and they crawled on.

As they made their way through the purple-and-yellow-striped pipe, Aiden could see other kids crawling, climbing, and sliding through the pipes to the left of the one he and Jace were in. On the right, the pipe's walls were mostly mirrored. Occasionally, though, a break in the mirroring gave Aiden a glimpse of a huge knotted network of pipes that appeared to be completely empty of kids.

After a few feet, the yellow-and-purple pipe started ascending slowly. They continued crawling. And they crawled. And they crawled.

The pipe went up gradually for a while and then leveled out. Aiden figured by then they were probably on the second-story level of the Pizzaplex. He thought they'd encounter a junction leading to other pipes, but they didn't. Instead, the yellow-and-purple pipe continued on, now sloping downward just as gradually as it had climbed upward.

The whole time they crawled, Aiden could see other kids in tubes to his left, but on his right, the pipe was either mirrored or overlooking the apparently deserted area. The pipe they were in appeared to encircle a section of the maze that no one else could get into.

Aiden wasn't sure how long they crawled before they found themselves right back where they'd started.

They recognized the spot because they could see the glow-in-the-dark balls in the pit at the base of the slide.

"Wow," Jace said. "That was a big circle. We crawled for fourteen minutes and forty-two seconds!"

Leave it to Jace to keep the time.

"Did we miss an offshoot?" Aiden asked.

Jace shook his head. "Besides the dark pipe, I didn't see any options."

Aiden cocked his head. "That means the part of the maze inside the circle we just made is like its own thing. Did you see that? No one was in those pipes."

"I noticed that."

"It would be great to check it out. There has to be a way to get to it."

"Well," Jace said, "if all those mirrors are partitions like you think, they're blocking the way. That means there's no way we can get in."

Aiden looked toward where they'd passed the black pipe opening. "Unless the dark tube leads into the area."

"Oh, right. It might."

"You want to go see?" Aiden asked.

"Sure."

This time, Jace took the lead. He crawled down the yellow-and-purple tube until they reached the dark off-shoot. There, he paused and looked over his shoulder.

"I'm with you," Aiden said.

Jace nodded and headed into the nearly blackened plastic pipe.

The dark pipe wasn't straight. It switched left, then right, and then left every few feet, like a back-and-forth trail going up a steep incline. The incline, however, wasn't steep enough to require the repeated turns. It was just as gradual as the one in the yellow-and-purple tube.

After a few minutes of this back-and-forth, Aiden figured they were again at the second-story level. Jace stopped. Aiden peered past Jace's shoulder. The dark pipe had dead-ended.

"That's weird," Jace said. "We've never found a dead end before."

Aiden scooted up next to Jace and put his hands against the smoky plastic. He peered through it. He could see the vague outlines of a convoluted matrix of pipes that was completely empty of kids. "I wonder why this area is blocked off."

"If it was for maintenance, wouldn't there be a mirror like the others?" Jace asked.

Aiden nodded. "You'd think."

Aiden spotted a join in the plastic. He prodded at it. When the plastic didn't give, he shifted so he could kick at the seam. Maybe if he could dent it, he could grab the edge of it and pull it back.

"What're you doing?" Jace asked.

"I want to see what's in this section. I mean, it has to be huge, and except for the openings blocked off by mirrors, this seems to be the only way in."

"But if it's sealed off here, maybe it's not safe."

Aiden made a face. "How unsafe could it be? We're in a pipe maze for little kids."

Jace pursed his lips as if considering the idea.

"Move back," Aiden said. "I need some room to maneuver."

Jace scooted backward, and Aiden got in position to kick at the partition. Leaning back on his hands, he booted the plastic with his right foot.

A sharp crack echoed through the pipe, and the seam between the pipe and the partition expanded . . . by about an eighth of an inch, if that. Aiden grunted and shifted again. He tried to stick his pinkie into the opening. The space wasn't big enough.

Aiden used the side of his fist to pound on the seam. It didn't give. He looked at Jace. "Can I borrow your knife?"

Jace dug out his Swiss Army knife. He fiddled with it, opening it to a file. "This might be the best tool." He handed the knife to Aiden.

Aiden stuck the file's tip into the seam between the pipe wall and the partition. He pushed the file in and attempted to pry the two apart.

It didn't work. He switched out the file for the knife itself, and he started stabbing at the partition. Maybe he could cut it open.

Nope, that didn't work, either. The plastic was too hard.

Aiden closed the knife and handed it back to Jace. He positioned himself so he could kick at the partition again. Jace backed up to give him room.

Aiden pummeled the partition with both feet this time. It didn't work any better than his one-foot assault had.

But maybe if he did it several times, it would weaken. Aiden braced himself and kicked again. And again.

Each time he kicked, the pipe they were in shook and wavered back and forth a little. But still, the partition remained in place.

Aiden repositioned, trying to get more leverage for a more powerful kick. Before he could unleash the kick, Jace tapped him on the shoulder. Aiden turned to find Happs smiling at him.

"Hello. I'm Happs. Are you lost?"

Aiden felt his cheeks flush. He knew he shouldn't have been doing what he'd been doing, and he'd been caught . . . by a robot, but still.

"Hi, Happs," Jace said innocently. "No, we're fine."

Happs's yellow eyes dimmed for an instant, then brightened again. His smile widened; his big teeth glowed. "You are lost. I will lead you out of Freddy's Fortress. Please come with me."

Happs reached out an oversize foam hand and tried to take Jace's arm.

"Hey!" Jace protested. He jerked his arm away from Happs.

"We're not lost," Aiden told Happs. "We don't need your help."

Happs ignored Aiden. "You are lost. I will lead you out of Freddy's Fortress. Please come with me."

Aiden rolled his eyes. "Yeah, we got that. Thanks, but no thanks. We're fine. I'm sorry we were messing with the wall here. We were just curious. But we're fine. We can find our way out."

Happs's smile brightened to a nearly blinding level of illumination. "You are lost. I will lead you out of

Freddy's Fortress. Please come with me." Once again, Happs reached for Jace.

Aiden quickly leaned forward between Happs and his friend. He threw his shoulder into Happs. The robot skidded back a few inches.

Aiden was surprised at how lightweight Happs was. Encouraged, he pushed at Happs with both hands. "Go on," Aiden said. "Go away. We're fine."

The light in Happs's eyes blinked several times. Happs appeared to look past Aiden and Jace, as if he was appraising the partition. Then Happs looked directly at Aiden. "You are lost. I will lead you—"

"Shut up!" Aiden shouted. He shoved Happs another time. Happs scooted away, but then he tried to churn closer again.

Aiden was fed up.

Aiden and Jace had liked Happs. They'd thought he was friendly. Now the robot was being as bossy as everyone else in Aiden's life. Aiden's head was suddenly filled with the voices of his parents and teachers and classmates: *Do this, Aiden. Don't do that, Aiden. Hurry up, Aiden. You're not doing that right, Aiden. You're a freak, Ai**don***.

With a shriek of frustration and rage, Aiden pulled his legs back and kicked out at Happs as hard as he could. Jace, his face red, as if he, too, had lost it, squirmed around so he could also kick at Happs. Together, the teens pounded on the robot with their feet, battering Happs back against the side of the pipe.

Happs made no effort to defend himself. His eyes remained bright, and he continued to smile. He kept smiling even when the teens' kicks cracked his plastic head and snapped Happs's arm joints, leaving his foam hands dangling. He also continued to smile when the pipe started to gyrate, swinging back and forth as if no longer anchored. And his smile went on when the pipe popped loose and plunged down into darkness.

Aiden landed on his back—hard. His head whacked something solid beneath him, a sharp flash of pain radiated down his spine. He groaned, and for a few seconds, he lay still while he tried not to panic. Had he broken anything?

Aiden tentatively moved his hands, then his arms and legs. Everything seemed to be working okay.

Moving slowly, Aiden felt around. His upper body still seemed to be in the plastic pipe. He could feel its smooth, curved sides. But he could also feel behind its sides. It appeared to have broken open when it fell.

Aiden elbowed himself up into a sitting position. "Jace?"

Aiden heard Jace groan. "Are you okay, Jace?"

Jace coughed. "Yeah, I just"—he noisily sucked in air—"I think I just got the wind knocked out of me."

Aiden blinked and looked around.

When they'd first started to fall, he'd felt like they were dropping into total blackness, but now he realized he could see his surroundings. The lighting was dim, but his eyes were adjusting to the shadows; he could tell they'd landed inside the area they'd been trying to reach.

Well, okay. This wasn't the most efficient way to get in, but they were in.

Aiden heard a scrape, and he looked over to see Jace sit up. Jace rotated his head to scan the area around them.

"Where's Happs?" Jace asked.

Aiden cringed. He'd forgotten about Happs.

He looked all around, too, but he didn't see the robot. Had Happs avoided the fall?

"Happs must not have fallen with us," Jace said.

Aiden looked up. Just as he did, he heard a hiss, and he watched what appeared to be a clear partition cover the space they'd just fallen through. He blinked. "Hey, Jace, look." He pointed at the clear partition.

Jace looked up. He frowned. "What is it?"

"A partition just slid into place up there, just like it did in that other pipe. But it's not a mirror. We can see through it. Look."

Jace rubbed his head, then tilted it to gaze upward.

"You know what?" Aiden said. "I think those mirrors are two-way. On the other side, it looks like a mirror, but in the closed-off area, it's like glass. See?"

Jace nodded.

Aiden looked around. "I think we're the only ones in this section."

"What about them?" Jace pointed.

Aiden looked in the direction of Jace's finger. Then he examined their surroundings again.

It appeared as if Aiden and Jace had fallen into a junction area in the closed-off web of pipes. Four corridors opened up off the junction, which was now sealed above them. Beyond the corridors, which were transparent like all the other pipes in the fortress, the main part of the maze was visible. Jace was pointing at a group of kids who appeared to be crawling past the junction just a few feet away. Obviously, though, the kids couldn't see them. The two-way mirror partitions hid Jace and Aiden from view.

Aiden carefully shifted onto his hands and knees. "Well, we might as well explore. We have this whole area to ourselves . . . and it's huge!" Aiden threw out a hand to indicate the separate area of the maze.

Jace grinned and nodded. He rubbed at a scrape on his elbow. "It's like our own town. Aiden-and-Jace-ville."

Aiden laughed. He gave Jace a playful punch. "You're such a dork."

"Yeah, and proud of it." Jace gazed at the pipe openings around them. "Which way do you want to go first?"

Aiden shrugged. "You pick. I don't think it matters. Let's just go and see where we end up."

"Works for me."

Aiden gestured for Jace to take the lead. Jace pointed at one of the openings, and the boys crawled into a glittery red pipe.

The red pipe led to a midnight-blue pipe, which led to a lime-green one. Some of the pipes went up. Some went down, some seemed to wind in concentric circles that returned them to where they started.

They climbed up ladder pipes. They scaled climbing pipes. They crawled left and right and straight.

The whole time they were exploring, they could see other kids in the pipes outside the separated area. Being apart from those kids made Aiden feel special. He liked it a lot.

At one point, when Jace paused to catch his breath, Aiden pointed at a tube that looked like it ascended gradually. "Let's go that way next. We might find a hidden slide."

"After you," Jace said.

Aiden led Jace into the ascending pipe, which was a deep golden color. Beyond the pipe, Aiden could see the roller-coaster track, and as he watched, the cars streaked past. As they continued to climb, he was able to look out at the rest of the Pizzaplex. The higher they got, the smaller the people down below looked. Being up here above their pint-size forms made Aiden feel important . . . or at least more important than he usually felt. This perspective of the people in the Pizzaplex had always been available to them in the maze, but somehow it was better now that Aiden knew they were invisible to the people outside the maze. He liked the anonymity it gave them.

The month before, Jace had asked Aiden what super-hero power he'd choose if he could have one. Flying? Amazing strength? Teleporting? X-ray vision? "I'd go for strength," Jace had said. "I'd be the amazing little strong guy." He'd laughed and pointed at Aiden. "Which power would you pick?"

"Invisibility," Aiden had answered without any thought at all. If he was invisible, he wouldn't be judged for how he looked, and he could go wherever he wanted to go. He'd be in control.

Being hidden in this section of the maze was kind of like that. He and Jace could go wherever they wanted inside the partitioned-off area. No one could see them do it. No one could stop them.

Aiden and Jace passed up every offshoot they encountered as they climbed up and up in a circuitous path to the highest level of the maze. They figured when they reached the top, they'd stay up there and look for a slide, but it took a while to reach the top because they stuck with the slowly ascending pipe instead of opting for a ladder pipe or a pipe with climbing holds. That was okay. They were in no hurry.

When the pipe they crawled through leveled out, they had the choice of three offshoots. The first one they chose meandered around on the upper level for a while before leading them, in a convoluted series of twists and turns, back to where they'd started. They tried the other offshoot, and it took them on a long loop around the deserted area. Eventually, though, the long loop hooked up with an intersecting pipe, and that one led to a slide.

At the top of the slide, which was made of burnt-orange plastic, Jace pointed at the steepness of its descent. "This one might go straight down," he said. "Might be the fastest one we've found."

Aiden grinned. "Let's find out."

Just as they had for the other slide, they positioned themselves in tandem, and Jace hung on to Aiden's belt loop. "Ready?" Aiden asked.

"Let 'er rip."

Aiden pushed off, and the boys shot downward so fast

that Aiden felt like they were falling off a cliff. For a second, his heart vaulted into his mouth, and adrenaline flooded his system.

The adrenaline ushered a chilling thought into Aiden's brain: What if this section wasn't finished? What would be at the bottom of the slide?

Thankfully, Aiden didn't have long to fret about this idea. The slide dropped them in a flash . . . but in the last instant, the slide leveled out, and they slipped off it, skidding across the slick curved bottom of a clear plastic pipe that extended across the bottom floor of the Pizzaplex. When their momentum ran out, they came to a stop at the juncture of two other pipes.

"Wow!" Jace breathed. "That was a rush!"

Aiden nodded. He shifted to his knees. As he did, his stomach growled. He looked at his watch.

"We've been in here for almost two hours, Jace. No wonder I'm hungry. It's been almost four hours since we ate that pizza."

Jace checked his own watch. "You're right." He dug in the pocket of his jeans, and he pulled out one of the fancy dark-chocolate-and-macadamia candy bars he liked. "Want half?"

Aiden looked at the crumpled bar. It wasn't exactly appetizing, but he nodded. "Thanks."

Aiden got into a cross-legged position next to Jace, who was still sitting with his legs splayed where he'd ended up after the slide. The two boys sat side by side in the pipe, eating the mostly melted chocolate and crunchy nuts. Through the two-way mirror, they could see into the dining area, which was full of happy families scarfing down pizzas and swilling soda. Trying to unstick part of a nut from his back teeth, Aiden realized how thirsty he was. Aiden fervently wished they could get to the dining area so they could have a soda and order another pizza.

As soon as he had that thought, another thought tumbled into his head. This one wasn't as nice as thinking about pizza and soda.

This thought, Aiden realized, was a disturbing cousin to the one he'd had on the slide. In fact, it was a thought that had been nagging at him ever since he'd wondered what might be at the bottom of the slide.

When Aiden had realized this part of the maze might not be finished—and he was glad he was wrong about that—another thought had popped into his head. What if this part of the maze was effectively closed off from the rest of it, so much so that they couldn't get out?

"Jace?" Aiden said, turning to look at his friend.

"Yeah?" Jace licked chocolate off his fingers.

"I think we might want to start looking for a way out of this section."

Jace got up on his hands and knees. "Oh, I've kind of been looking already. Actually, I thought the slide might take us out. I figured the way out has to be on the bottom of the maze or the top. We pretty much went entirely around the middle of it when we found it."

"True."

"But the slide didn't do it."

"Ya think?" Aiden winked at his friend.

Jace rolled his eyes. "I'm thirsty. Let's find a way out."

Aiden got on his hands and knees. He winced. Not only was his back still sore from the fall, his knees were starting to protest all the crawling.

Jace groaned when he got to his knees, too. "Sure wish we had some kneepads."

Aiden laughed. "Yeah, that would be nice." He took a deep breath. "Any ideas of how to find an exit?"

"You're the thinker," Jace said. "What do you think we should do?"

Aiden considered their alternatives. Finally, he said, "Let's try to be systematic. Explore every main pipe and try each offshoot one by one. What do you think?"

Jace gazed out at the enclosure of entwined pipes. "This place is big, but it's not that big. We should be able to find the way out if we do that."

Aiden couldn't miss the doubt in Jace's voice. Jace clearly wasn't sure he believed what he was saying. Aiden understood. He had similar concerns. If this part of the maze was deserted, that must mean it was sealed off. And if it was sealed off, that probably meant it had no exit.

But maybe Aiden was wrong.

"You can lead," Jace said. "Your memory is better than mine. You can keep track of where we've been and where we haven't been."

Aiden nodded and set off ahead of Jace. Envisioning everywhere they'd explored so far, he led Jace to the left, heading toward a pipe they hadn't yet tried. From there, he attempted to make their trek through the pipes as sequential as possible, ticking off the sections on a mental checklist as they went.

Unfortunately, Aiden wasn't wrong. No matter how many turns, ascents, and descents they made, they couldn't find a way out of the partitioned–off area.

It was Jace who admitted defeat first. When they'd retraced their path along a main pipe for the second time, Jace said, "Hold up."

Aiden stopped and looked at his friend.

Jace sat back on his butt. "We're trapped in here, aren't we?"

Aiden got off his knees and sat, too. He leaned against the curved wall of the pipe. He let his head drop against the plastic.

Aiden gazed through the other side of the pipe. Beyond it, he could see a little girl riding a Freddy replica on the carousel. The little girl's head was thrown back. Even though Aiden couldn't hear her, he knew she was laughing.

"Aiden?"

Aiden shifted his gaze to Jace. He noticed that a vein at Jace's temple was throbbing at a strobe-like pace. Aiden realized his heart was matching the rhythm. They were both scared.

"Yeah, Jace. I think we're trapped."

Aiden could hear Jace's breathing quicken. The vein pulsed even faster. Jace's eyes filled with tears. He quickly wiped his face with the back of his hand.

Aiden wanted to tell Jace it was okay if he wanted to cry because Aiden wanted to cry, too. But he couldn't get his mouth to work.

Aiden cleared his throat and licked his lips. He opened

his mouth, but before he could speak, a muffled scratching sound stopped him.

Jace inhaled sharply and spun around to look toward the sound. "What was that?"

Aiden frowned and shook his head. Both he and Jace cocked their heads, listening intently.

At first, they heard nothing, but then a distant scrape was followed by a faint crackle of static. Both boys tensed. Neither made a sound.

For several more seconds, they listened. Then Jace exhaled. Aiden realized he'd been holding his breath, too. He let it out.

Jace glanced over at Aiden. "Do we want to think about what that was?"

Aiden shook his head. "Better to think about how to get out of here."

Jace nodded. He rubbed his face. "Okay, let's think this through."

"Okay."

"We've been looking for an exit, and we haven't found one."

"Thank you, Mr. Obvious."

Jace winced.

"Sorry, Jace. I'm not at my best."

"I get it."

Several seconds of silence passed. Finally, Aiden encouraged Jace to continue. "Go on. You sounded like you were leading up to an idea."

Jace sighed. "Well, it's not a very good one."

"A not very good one is better than none at all. And I've got nothing."

Jace bit his lower lip. Then he leaned forward. "Okay, so we know there's an opening on the second level, where we were trying to get through that partition. What if we can find our way back there, and we work at that seam some more? That partition might have weakened when the pipe fell. We weren't able to pry it open from the other side, but maybe we could from this side."

Aiden frowned. "But the pipe on the other side of that seam is what fell. We'd have nowhere to go from there even if we got through the partition."

Jace shook his head. "The part of the pipe that fell was only three feet or so long. If we could get the partition loose, we could use it as a bridge to cross that opening."

"Well, we might be able to pry the partition open, but what if we can't get it completely loose?" Aiden asked.

Jace twisted his mouth. "Well, we might be able to swing ourselves across, like hang from the pipe on one side and then swing over to the other. Like on the bars in gym class."

Aiden thought about the idea. It was pretty weak. He and Jace were ridiculously unathletic, and even if they were strong and coordinated, broken climbing pipes were different from gymnastic bars.

But did Aiden have anything better? Before Aiden could respond, Jace gave Aiden a weak grin as he pulled out his Swiss Army knife. "And I still have my mighty sword."

Aiden laughed. He painfully returned to his knees. "Okay, Sir Jace. Let's do it. Lead on."

Jace tried to keep his grin in place as he also returned to his knees. Aiden pretended the grin was effective, and he pretended he didn't hear Jace's occasional whimpers as Jace led them quickly back to the spot Aiden had tried to break through before they had fallen into this area.

Although getting to the right place wasn't a problem, finding the seam took a little effort. It was, after all, just the narrowest of slits in the plastic along one short section of pipe. Both Aiden and Jace had to feel their way along the wall of the pipe to find it.

As soon as they located the seam, Jace pulled out his knife. Flipping out the main blade, he began sawing along the scant opening that Aiden had created earlier.

Aiden could do nothing but watch. He had no knife of his own.

After a few minutes, Jace dropped his hand. "It's not working." He wiped his eyes again.

Aiden leaned past Jace's shoulder to examine the opening. Then he leaned closer still. His heart did a little stutter step of hope.

"Actually, yes, it is," he said. "Look." Aiden pointed to a series of fine stress fractures along the opening. Whether Jace had made them with his knife or they'd been created when the pipe collapsed, Aiden didn't know. He did, however, think—or hope—that the stress fractures might have weakened the joint enough that he might be able to kick the partition free.

When Jace spotted the stress fractures, his eyes lit up. "Do you think . . . ?" He didn't finish the thought.

"Back up. My legs are longer. I'll do the kicking."

Jace nodded and scooted out of the way.

Aiden took up position on his butt, propped backward on his hands. He pulled in his legs as tight to his body as he could get them so he could coil up with as much power as possible. Then he thrust his feet out hard and fast.

Crack!

The plastic protested the impact, but it held.

Aiden didn't care. He pulled his knees in, and he kicked out again. And again.

Breathing hard, Aiden paused after the third kick. He sat forward and looked at the seam. The cracks extended farther from the opening. He was getting somewhere. He set up to kick some more.

On the sixth kick, the plastic gave in. The partition popped loose at the seam, and it swung open like a miniature doorway.

Behind Aiden, Jace shouted, "Yes!"

Aiden grinned. Panting, he sat forward and started to grasp the partition. Surely, they'd be able to free it from the other side of the opening, too.

"Help me," Aiden said.

Jace scooted up beside Aiden. He started to reach for the plastic. Then he stopped. His hand dropped. He made a little choking sound in his throat.

Aiden turned to look at Jace. "What's wrong?"

Jace pointed.

Aiden immediately saw what Jace had already seen.

Although Jace had been right that the gap between the partition and the intact pipe was small enough to get across, there was an insurmountable problem on the other side: one of the two-way mirror partitions had been put into place on the far side of the gap. There was no way past that.

Aiden collapsed onto his back, utterly defeated. Jace slumped next to him.

"Sorry, Aiden," Jace said. "It was a dumb idea."

Aiden shook his head. "No, it was . . ." He stopped.

From farther along the pipe they were in, a whirring sound was coming their way. Aiden sat up.

"Is that Happs?" he asked.

Jace cocked his head and listened. The whirring sound was interspersed with a thud and a scrape. "If it is, he doesn't sound the way he normally sounds."

Aiden stared down the pipe. Jace was right. The robot sounded clunky, like he was damaged.

The robot's noisy approach got louder. The boys gazed down the length of the tube, waiting.

Aiden realized he was holding his breath, and he quietly let it out. Beside him, Jace was trembling and breathing in sharp gasps.

Why was Jace afraid? Wasn't Happs programmed to help kids in the maze? Broken or not, couldn't he get them out? Shouldn't they have been eager to see Happs?

Jace got to his knees and aimed himself in the opposite direction from Happs's approach. "We need to get out of here, Aiden," he whispered. His words came out so fast they ran together.

It took Aiden a second to process what Jace said. In that second, the danger that Jace had intuited became clear.

From around a bend in the pipe just a few feet away, Happs appeared. And he did not look happy.

His face cracked, one of his eyes dark, and the yellow security light on top of his head sheered away, Happs's signature smile was in place; the smile, however, was incomplete. Half of his glowing teeth were gone, and his up-curved mouth had been shattered on one side. This turned his cheerful expression into a malevolent sneer. Even though Happs's metal torso appeared to be unscathed, the robot no longer looked friendly.

As soon as Happs spotted the boys, he spoke . . . sort of. His programming had obviously been damaged because only a portion of his usual spiel came through. What he said was, "Lost. Out. With me."

The words had staticky gaps separating them, and they weren't spoken in Happs's usual sprightly tone. Happs's high-pitched voice had dropped a couple octaves. His tones were low and guttural; they sounded threatening.

It wasn't Happs's words that kicked the boys into gear, though. It was his hands.

Jace shouted, "Come on!" as he began crawling madly away from Happs. Aiden didn't hesitate. He crawled as fast as he could in Jace's wake.

Behind the boys, Happs clattered and scraped his way along. Each scrape made Aiden flinch. His whole body was wound into a knot of tense terror.

As Aiden and Jace scrabbled through the tube, Aiden

thought about the foam hands that had always made Happs look so harmless and helpful. Those hands . . . were gone.

Probably ripped free when the pipe fell, the foam was no longer there to conceal the metallic workings they'd covered. Without the foam, the robot's spiky metal pincers were exposed.

But in the few seconds Aiden had looked at Happs, he realized the missing foam hands weren't what made the robot a threat. The pincers had been sheared off as well. Instead of mechanisms that could grip and be useful, Happs now had lethal metal shards at the end of his arms. His arm joints were damaged as well, so each articulation was jagged. His friendly-looking arms had morphed into threatening metal extensions protruding from his torso, and he was flailing the menacing sharp edges as the extensions stabbed and slashed at the pipe walls he passed.

"This way!" Jace shouted. He took a left into a descending tube.

Before Aiden pushed off to scoot down after Jace, he turned to check on Happs. The mangled robot was rolling toward him, about fifteen feet away.

Thankfully, Happs wasn't moving at his full speed. Aiden realized this was because one of Happs's treads was hanging partially off its runner, and the other rolling track was askew; this was causing Happs to lurch consistently to his right. The other track was working to put Happs back in the direction Happs wanted to go, but the constant oppositional yank and pull made for much slower progress than the robot should have been capable of.

Slower, though, was a relative term. In just the few seconds that Aiden spent examining Happs's progress, Happs had almost managed to get within arm's reach of Aiden.

Aiden quickly flipped from his knees onto his butt. Pushing off with his hands, he propelled himself down the sloping pipe, wishing as he did that the slope was steeper. Although the pipe descended—like a slide—it was an anemic slide, probably intended for the smaller kids who were afraid of the steep, fast slides.

Ahead of Aiden, Jace was also on his butt, his legs straight out in front of him. He was using his hands to push off the bottom of the pipe, attempting to scoot faster than gravity alone allowed. Aiden mimicked Jace's movements.

Behind him, a metallic thunk made a spot between Aiden's shoulder blades tingle. His imagination provided him with a frighteningly clear image of Happs's honed metal spearing Aiden in the back. Aiden was afraid the downward cant of the pipe would give Happs more speed than Jace and Aiden were managing.

It didn't help that Happs was now repeating the same thing he'd said when they'd first spotted him a few minutes before.

"Lost. Out. With me," Happs kept saying. Unnerving crackling surrounded each word.

Aiden realized he'd been more in his head than in the pipe when his feet suddenly encountered Jace's butt. Forcing himself not to think about the pursuing robot, Aiden focused on his friend and realized that Jace was scrambling onto his knees. The descending tube had ended.

"I see a ladder pipe!" Jace shouted. "He's slower on the ladders. Come on!"

"Good thinking," Aiden said as he, too, repositioned himself onto his knees.

Sparing a glance behind him, still convinced that impalement was a likely possibility any second, Aiden gasped. He was right. The end of Happs's cutting-edge "hands" were just a couple feet from Aiden's side.

Aiden yelped, lunged after Jace, and groped for the highest rung on the ladder he could reach. He pulled his legs up as fast as he could and scrabbled up the ladder behind Jace, who was climbing like a monkey with its tail on fire.

The ladder wasn't long—maybe twenty feet at the most. When Aiden reached the top of it, he found Jace frowning at the two pipe openings available to them. Both of them appeared to be level pipes.

"Lost. Out. With me." Happs's garbled words echoed up from the bottom of the ladder pipe.

Aiden pulled his legs off the ladder and looked down. He exhaled in relief.

Happs was still at the bottom of the ladder. Because Happs had always used his foam hands to grip the rungs and those foam hands were missing, the robot could only swipe at the rungs. His swipes were carving up the rungs, cutting them away from the pipe walls.

Apparently aware that his hands weren't working right, Happs thrust out his third limb, the telescoping extender that came from his middle. He tried to use it to grab on to one of the rungs he'd cut up, but the extender wasn't functioning, either . . . at least not as anything that could grip. It, too, had been damaged, and it now looked more like a serrated knife than a cleaning tool.

That additional deadly weapon wasn't good, Aiden thought. But at least Happs didn't have a way to climb up after the boys.

"Which way do you think?" Jace asked.

Aiden turned and looked at Jace's tight red face. Jace's face was smeared with tear tracks. Aiden pretended not to notice.

"I have no idea. It may not matter. If we stay on this level, we might be okay. Look." Aiden pointed at Happs, who was trying and failing to grab a ladder rung.

Jace hesitated, clearly not wanting to move even an inch closer to where Happs was. Then he creeped up next to Aiden and looked down the ladder pipe. Aiden felt Jace's taut muscles loosen—slightly, and he heard Jace exhale.

Aiden started to turn to examine the two pipes leading away from the top of the ladder pipe, but Jace grabbed his arm. Aiden turned back.

"Aiden, look!"

Aiden glanced at Jace, who was still staring intently at the bottom of the ladder pipe. Aiden shifted his gaze in that direction, just in time to watch one of the two-way mirrored safety panels sliding into place above Happs.

A swish and a click, and Happs was no longer in view. Jace and Aiden were now looking at reflections of themselves in the mirrored surface of a safety door. In spite of the situation, Aiden couldn't help but notice neither he nor Jace were looking their best.

Aiden sat back on his heels and tried to smooth his hair, which he now knew was even more crazed than usual. He wiped the slick sheen of sweat from his dirty face, careful to avoid his swollen eye—the area around it was now a deep, dark purple.

Jace, too, scrubbed at his face; he'd probably seen the tear tracks on his cheeks. "I'm not sure if that partition is a good thing or a bad thing," he said.

Aiden nodded. "I get you. On the one hand, Happs can't climb up here after us. On the other hand, if those safety doors are closing off wherever he's been, we're going to have less and less room to maneuver. I didn't think much about it at the time—I was too busy thinking about getting away; but the pipe behind Happs was pretty torn up. He must be damaging things right and left."

Jace frowned and nodded. "So, what do we do?"

Aiden had no idea. He looked at the two pipe openings. Which one would keep them away from Happs?

Jace nudged Aiden. "You have a better memory than I do. Can you remember any of the layout in here?"

"I've been trying to picture it in my head, but it's kind of a blur. Give me a second to think."

Jace nodded and closed his eyes as if he could make the problem disappear by not seeing it.

Aiden leaned back against the pipe wall, but instead of

thinking about the maze's layout, he looked out through the two-way mirror that separated them from the rest of the Pizzaplex. They were so close to help.

Below them, just beyond the pipe they were in, two young boys were being strapped into the giant swings. Both boys were redheads, probably brothers; they had identical grins. They were having so much fun. Past them, Aiden could see the bumper cars zipping this way and that. Although the scene was blurred because of the layers of colored plastic separating the tubes from the bumper car arena, Aiden was pretty sure Nora and her friends were in four of the cars. They were ramming several cars driven by guys in letter jackets. It was a whole other world . . . Not just the bumper cars, but the social circle that enveloped kids like Nora and her friends. Aiden had always wondered what it would be like to have a place in a network like that.

"Aiden?"

Aiden pulled his gaze from the distant bumper cars. He looked at Jace.

Jace, too, was now gazing at the kids having fun outside the maze. Suddenly, Jace got up on his knees, faced the pipe's wall, and started pounding on the sides of the pipe. "Help!" he screamed. "Help us! We're stuck in here! Hey! Help!"

Jace's panic was infectious. Aiden started pounding on the plastic, too. "Help!" he bellowed at the top of his lungs. "We're in here! Help us!"

Aiden wasn't sure how long they hammered at the

plastic with their fists and shouted as loud as they could. It could have been seconds or hours. It was probably at least a few minutes because when Aiden's last "Help!" broke into a rasp, he realized his throat was on fire. His fists throbbed.

Aiden put his head in his hands. Jace was still shouting, but his voice was getting hoarse. His strikes on the plastic were weakening.

Aiden touched Jace's arm. Jace whipped around. Spittle dripped from the sides of his mouth. His face was red from exertion.

"They can't hear us," Aiden said. "Too much sound muffling in here and too much noise out there."

Jace wiped his mouth. He opened it like he was going to argue, but then he exhaled loudly. "I know." Flopping back on his butt, Jace looked away from Aiden; he was trying to pull himself together.

They sat in silence for a few seconds. Finally, Jace cleared his throat. He turned to face Aiden. "Have you figured it out?"

Aiden sighed. He hadn't figured anything out. He'd been too busy pointlessly yelling his head off.

Yes, he remembered the maze's layout pretty well, but that didn't do them a lot of good. He shrugged and pointed at one of the pipes. "I think if we take the left pipe there, it will keep us on this level." He dropped his hand. "But the trouble is, what good does that do us? Are we just going to crawl back and forth until our knees are bloody? It's not like there's a way out up here. And"—he gestured at the kids and adults outside the maze—"they can't see us or hear us. I'm wondering if we should just stay here. Maybe someone will come looking for us."

"Like who?" Jace's question was almost whispered, as if he barely had the strength to ask it. "Our parents?" His mouth twisted.

"Good point."

Aiden tried to think of something helpful to say.

Jace beat him to it. "Actually, maybe you're right. Maybe the Fazbear Entertainment people, you know, workers, will find us. Wouldn't they send someone in to repair the pipes?"

"Eventually."

Jace was silent. He stared at his sneakers. "Eventually," he repeated. His face was pale.

Aiden nodded. He had a feeling his face was as pale as Jace's.

Aiden pressed his hands against the pale blue plastic beneath them. "I don't think we should stay here. Happs may not be able to climb ladders, but all he has to do is find an ascending pipe, and he'll get up to this level eventually. If we stay here, he could box us in."

Jace nodded. "I remember a couple of junctions where there were like at least four offshoots. If we got to one of those, we could rest and think some more. We'd have multiple escape routes if Happs finds us."

"Good idea." Aiden used his chin to gesture at the left pipe opening. "I think that one will get us to one of those junctions."

Jace nodded.

Aiden cringed as he pushed himself up onto his knees. When Jace didn't move, Aiden turned to look at his friend.

Jace stared down at the bumper cars. "I wish we'd taken out our frustration with the cars instead of coming in here."

"Yeah, you and me both." Aiden crawled toward the left pipe opening. He assumed Jace would follow him . . . which he did.

The pipe they entered went straight for fifty feet or so, but then it took a big, gradual turn and started heading downward. Aiden didn't want to go down, so he quickly looked for an alternative route. When he spotted one, he turned that way. But he was brought up short in just a couple feet. They were blocked by one of the two-way mirror safety barriers.

Aiden gestured at the barrier. "I don't remember that being here when we passed by here earlier." He looked around. "I remember this pipe." It was a distinctive pipe—aqua with multicolored polka dots.

Jace nodded. "I do, too. And no, that wasn't here."

Aiden frowned. "That means Happs was close by. He damaged more tubes, and they were closed off."

"That's not good."

Aiden looked toward another offshoot. "We can go this way, but I'm pretty sure it goes to a part of the maze that isn't connected to the main conduits. If we can't get to a main conduit, our options are going to be limited."

"Yeah, I figured that." Jace looked down the offshoot. "Want to try it anyway? We still might be able to find a junction where we can watch for Happs." Jace licked his lips. "I sure wish I had some water."

"Me too." Aiden sighed. "Yeah, we might as well go that way." He pointed at the offshoot and started crawling in that direction. "You with me?"

Jace nodded.

Aiden continued on. He could hear Jace shuffle close behind.

Nora let out a shriek when Wyatt's bright orange car hurtled into the side of Nora's hot pink one. His car hit hers so hard that the impact literally rattled her teeth. Her head jerked far enough to the left that her earring gouged her neck.

"Hey!" she protested.

Wyatt didn't hear her. Not only was the hum of all the bumper cars loud but the rock music blasting from the arena's speakers was even louder. Her voice was lost in the racket.

Wyatt grinned at her. She gave him her best fuming, dirty look . . . which didn't bother him at all. He winked and turned his car to go after someone else.

Nora clenched her steering wheel and stomped on her accelerator, heading after Wyatt. She needed some payback.

Whizzing past a couple of her friends, Nora kept Wyatt in her sights as she aimed toward the arena's short outside wall. She intended to skirt past the melee in the middle and sneak up on Wyatt.

As she scooted along the wall, Nora glanced over the top of the wall. Beyond it, she could see a labyrinth of dark plastic pipes that extended into darkness in the distance. Something about the tangled plastic gave Nora the heebie-jeebies. She wondered what was back there.

A scream pulled her attention to the arena. Out in front of her, Wyatt and his friends were ganging up on some smaller kids, who were having trouble controlling their cars.

Nora forgot all about the pipes as she stomped on her accelerator. She focused on Wyatt and aimed right at him.

Aiden lost track of the number of pipes he and Jace wound through before they finally found a big junction that gave them a reasonable line of sight down every approaching tube. The multiple openings would provide several escape routes and would allow the boys to hear better. The more open the maze was, the less the pipes muted sound.

Aiden shifted into a sitting position. Jace did the same.

Aiden pointed at the various openings in turn. "That one is a ladder down. I don't think it's going to be a good option. Happs could just fling himself down after us." He pointed to the next two openings. "Those are level, so we could go that way, but Happs could probably come after us pretty easily." He pointed at the last opening. "I think going up that climbing pipe will be best. We already know Happs can't do ladders, and I don't see how he could do climbing pipes without his foam hands."

Jace looked at the climbing pipe opening. "But what's up there? How do we know it won't be another blocked-off area?"

Aiden crawled to the opening and looked up the

ladder. He exhaled loudly. "It looks clear." He returned to his sitting position. He rubbed his knees.

The boys didn't speak for several minutes. Finally, Jace broke the silence. "I feel bad about kicking Happs."

"I feel bad about a lot of things."

Jace stared at his feet. Then he looked up at Aiden. "Do you think robots are vindictive?"

Aiden made a face. "What? You think Happs is trying to get back at us for kicking him? You think he turned his arms into weapons so he can exact bloody revenge?" Aiden gave Jace an *are-you-kidding-me?* look. "Happs is high tech, but he's a robot. Robots don't feel. Therefore, they can't be vindictive."

Jace's mouth drooped. "Yeah, of course you're right. I'm being dumb."

Aiden punched Jace's arm. "You're never dumb. You're the smartest person I know."

"And you know, like, what, five people?"

Aiden laughed. "Good point." He sobered and poked Jace. "But I mean it. You're smart."

"Not smart enough to get us out of here."

Aiden shook his head. "We'll figure something out."

Although he'd tried to put confidence into the words when he spoke them, as soon as they were out of his mouth, Aiden could hear the lie. He realized that he didn't believe what—

A screeching scrape cut into Aiden's thoughts. The scrape was followed by a series of clunks. And then the distorted robotic voice. "Out. With me."

Jace stiffened. His eyes were huge.

Aiden figured his eyes were just as big. His heart had started racing.

"Out. With me," Happs repeated.

Sometime since they'd last seen him, Happs had lost more of his verbal functioning. Where *lost* had been, only a gravelly growl preceded the word *out*. But *out* sounded even more alarming than it had before. The command wasn't so much spoken in Happs's now contorted voice as it was barked like it was being shouted by an irate dictator, one with the means to execute his subjects.

Aiden managed to get his legs working. Kneeling, he scrambled to the climbing pipe opening. When Jace didn't move—when he continued to stare in the direction of Happs's approach, Aiden nudged him with the toe of his boot. "Come on!"

Jace blinked and got on his knees. He crawled into the climbing pipe behind Aiden. Aiden reached for the first handhold. As fast as he could, he pulled himself up and found a foothold. Then he reached for the next handhold and the next and the next. He crawled up the wall like a spider fleeing a ravenous bird. He didn't turn to look, but it sounded like Jace was right behind him.

As they'd hoped, the climbing tube ended up at an open fork leading to two level pipes. As Aiden stopped to evaluate his choices, his shoulders tightened. Happs's insistent warped reflection seemed to bounce back and forth up the climbing pipe behind them. Aiden risked a look as Happs repeated his insistent "Out. With me."

The words echoed through the climbing pipe and seemed to radiate outward into the other tubes.

As soon as Aiden checked on Happs, he was sorry he had. Although Happs hadn't been able to manage the ladder pipe, he was having better luck with the climbing pipe. His knifelike hands were slashing at the pipe's walls, but his mutilated treads still had enough functionality to find purchase on the hand- and footholds. Happs's progress was thankfully slow, but it was still progress. He was scaling the climbing tube.

"Come on!" Aiden led Jace into the left pipe.

They scurried along the pipe as fast as they could, but when they rounded its first bend, they realized they'd chosen the wrong pipe. It was blocked with a two-way mirror security barrier.

"Turn around!" Aiden shouted to Jace as soon as he saw the barrier. "Turn around!"

Jace turned around, but he was panting in terror. Aiden understood why. Had Happs made it to the top of the climbing pipe? If he had, they'd be crawling right into the sharp metal shards that used to be Happs's hands.

But what choice did they have?

"Faster!" Aiden urged Jace. He was nearly shoving Jace down the pipe. Aiden's long legs gave him more speed than Jace's short ones. And Jace was slowing, clearly reluctant to face what might be waiting at the end of the pipe.

Aiden shoved Jace out of the way and squeezed past him. He figured he had a better chance of facing off against Happs than Jace did.

Seconds after Aiden took the lead, they reached the junction again. At the same exact moment, the spear-like tip of Happs's left arm scored a gash in the junction's floor. The ripping sound made Happs's whirring and clanking even more hideous. Aiden felt like they were in the bowels of churning machinery designed to disassemble and pulverize whatever was put into it.

As Happs's now-serrated extender arm flailed toward Aiden, he flatted himself on the bottom of the pipe. His gaze darted around. Behind Happs, a security mirror was sliding over the top of the climbing pipe. That way was no longer an option. They couldn't go back the way they'd just come because it went nowhere. And Happs was blocking the only other pipe entrance.

Aiden looked up at Happs's gleaming metal arms. He froze when the arms started reaching for him.

Suddenly, Jace let out a banshee yell.

Lunging over the top of Aiden, Jace dove under Happs's outstretched arms. His Swiss Army knife in his fist, Jace jammed the blade into the open doorway in Happs's torso.

Jace's attack on Happs galvanized Aiden. He knew Jace's little knife wasn't going to do much damage to Happs's circuits, but he remembered that the little robot didn't weigh that much. Maybe they could drive him back . . . if they could avoid getting slashed.

Jace pulled his knife back and barely avoided getting stabbed when Happs jerked toward him. Aiden quickly flipped to his side and spun; he scissor-kicked Happs, shoving the robot against the junction's wall.

Realizing what Aiden was trying to do, Jace lay flat and added his kicks to the attack. Between the two of them, they managed to shove Happs into the dead-end pipe. And they were able to knock him over.

When Happs landed on his side, Aiden got to his knees. *Maybe we can finish him off*, Aiden thought. They should attack instead of fleeing. If they could get the plastic shell off his head, they might be able to rip out his circuitry. He fleetingly asked himself why he'd mastered juggling, Hula-Hooping, jump-roping, and yo-yoing. What good did those talents do him now? It wasn't like he could pull a juggling pin out of his back pocket and whack Happs in the face with it.

Jace must have had the same attack idea that Aiden had. He, too, shifted to his knees. His mouth was set, and his jaw bunched; he was ready for battle. Together, the two boys advanced on the thrashing robot.

They didn't get far.

Happs might have been on his side, but his arms hadn't stopped moving. He waved them continuously, which effectively turned him into a robotic propeller. Shining, sharp metal sliced through the air in turbulent sweeps that were impossible to completely avoid.

One of Happs's swipes caught Aiden on the cheek. Hot pain seared his skin, and warm blood ran down his jaw. He jerked his head back.

"Go, Aiden!" Jace shouted. He pointed at the other pipe opening. "We need to get away while we can!"

As Jace spoke, Happs suddenly whirred loudly and flipped up onto his treads.

"Go!" Jace urged again.

Aiden didn't argue. He turned around and crawled pell-mell into the other available pipe opening. Checking over his shoulder, Aiden saw that Jace was right behind him.

And Happs was right behind Jace. The robot had wasted no time reorienting himself. "Out. With me," he chanted as he rolled erratically after them.

This pipe was unfortunately a level pipe. Although Aiden and Jace were racing through it as fast as they could, Happs was having no trouble keeping up. The sounds of his humming motor and crunching treads chased the boys down the pipe.

Aiden's mouth went dry at the thought of how close Happs's jagged metal limbs must have been getting to Jace's feet. The image of that metal piercing Jace's sneakers or his skin gave Aiden the strength to crawl even faster.

The pipe took a sharp left turn, and then it switched back immediately to the right. After the abrupt right, it jogged left again. At the end of the left jog, the pipe opened to a platform.

It was the top of a slide!

Aiden lunged onto the platform. At the same time, he reached back and grabbed Jace by the shirt. He yanked Jace into his arms just as Happs lurched toward them, his deadly bladelike appendages sweeping the air only a few inches away from them.

"Hold on to me!" Aiden shouted. He pushed off the platform with every bit of strength he had.

The slide they'd found was a good one. It had a couple

turns, but mostly it was steep and straight. In just a matter of seconds, it shot them into a ball pit similar to the one they'd landed in just a couple hours earlier.

Aiden could only hope the few seconds it had taken to get to the pit had been enough. He had a sinking feeling it hadn't been. But he didn't have time to think about his dread.

As soon as they hit the plastic orbs, both Aiden and Jace started beating the balls aside, lunging their way through the colorful, spherical sea. Aiden had his eye on a pipe opening at the other side of the pit.

Unfortunately, though, they didn't reach it before Happs reached them.

As Aiden's foreboding had predicted, Happs had come down the slide just as fast—probably even faster—than Aiden and Jace had. And when he'd come off the slide, maybe because he was more compact, Happs had been launched farther out into the pit than the boys had been.

Happs also had no trouble plowing his way through the plastic balls. His mass shoved the balls aside like they were nothing.

This was why Happs got to them before Aiden and Jace could get out of the ball pit. And because Aiden was in the lead, Happs got to Jace first.

"Out. With me," Happs crackled as he reached out to grab his quarry.

Jace must have sensed that Happs was right behind him because he immediately dove into the ball pit as if it was a lake and he could skim under its surface to get away.

It would have been a decent plan, probably, if his feet hadn't popped up when he dove down.

Happs's limbs were extended in his efforts to grab Jace, when Jace's feet rose up out of the ball pit. Happs immediately tried to clutch the feet. But of course, his hands couldn't clutch. They could only slice.

The razor-like spikes at the ends of Happs's arms cut right through one of Jace's ankles, hacking off Jace's right foot roughly and crudely and with so much force that the foot was torn free of Jace's ankle and spit aside as if by a chain saw. The second the foot landed among the plastic balls with a plop, Jace's upper body erupted from the ball pit. Jace's mouth was opened wide in a shriek that was so loud and so high-pitched, Aiden wouldn't have been surprised if it had cracked nearby mirrored partitions.

Aiden immediately reached for Jace, grabbing at his friend's arm. He wasn't thinking. He had no plan. He was just reacting.

The problem was that Happs was doing the same thing. And it was faster than Aiden.

When Jace's chest appeared from under the heaving ball pit, Happs grabbed for Jace again. The robot's now-bloody knife-hands slashed through Jace's shoulder, and Jace's shrieks ratcheted even higher.

Aiden managed to hang on to Jace's forearm. Pulling with all his might, Aiden hitched Jace from the pit.

As soon as Jace was out of the pit, Aiden hooked his arms under Jace's armpits. Then he levered himself into the nearest pipe. He didn't know if it was too late to save his friend, but he had to try.

In just the few seconds since Jace's foot was amputated, he must have lost a massive amount of blood. Aiden had to get Jace away from Happs or it was going to be too late.

"Out. With me," Happs persisted.

Aiden yanked Jace farther into the pipe. Jace continued to scream in pain. His eyes were bulging impossibly wide, and his mouth was stretched into a grimace.

"Hang on, Jace!" Aiden shouted. He threw himself backward along the pipe, hauling Jace with him.

But, again, he wasn't fast enough.

Happs moved too quickly, and as he moved, he kept trying to get ahold of Jace. The shrill sound of metal on metal filled Aiden's ears as Happs brought both limbs together around Jace's lower body.

Aiden was sure Happs was trying to pick up Jace, but of course his torn metal couldn't do that. All it could do was slice and shred.

Aiden couldn't see what Happs was doing to Jace, but he could hear his bawling cries, and he could see Jace's face. It was so misshapen by pain that it was almost unrecognizable. Aiden tried to hold his friend's gaze, willing him to stay alive.

Behind Jace, the robot reached out again. "With me," Happs repeated

Aiden pushed off the floor of the pipe with all his strength. Clutching his friend, he heaved himself backward, trying to snatch Jace out of Happs's range.

But he couldn't do it.

Happs thrashed forward, and Jace howled. As he did, blood poured from his mouth.

Jace's eyes blinked once. Aiden felt Jace's body stiffen in his arms. Then he felt Jace go limp. Jace's eyes stared . . . at nothing.

Aiden, frozen in disbelief and shock, held on to Jace's body. He locked his gaze on Happs.

"Out. With me," Happs said.

Aiden had no choice. He let go of Jace and crawled like a demon down the pipe.

The next several seconds were nothing more than a confusion of sound and sensation for Aiden. He couldn't make sense of anything he was experiencing. He was vaguely aware that he was crawling for his life, but that thought was just a dim perception that was outweighed by all the other information assaulting his overloaded brain.

As if cascading down on him all at once, he felt tears spilling down his cheeks, bile filling his throat, snot dripping from his nose, sweat trickling down his back, blood pounding through his veins, and pain flashing in his knees. Woven through all that, overwhelming grief made him want to howl like an enraged wolf. Underneath these primitive reactions, his mind could only offer one repeated thought: *This can't be happening. This can't be happening. This can't be happening.*

Aiden's peripheral senses were working enough for him to be aware when Happs got close. He heard the metallic shredding sounds, and he registered the relentless whirring and the endless chant of "Out. With me."

Putting on as much speed as he could, Aiden shot through the pipe and found himself in another junction. Three of the pipe openings in the junction were partitioned off. He had just one option. Thankfully, it was a ladder pipe.

Just as Happs emerged from the pipe behind Aiden, Aiden scrambled up the ladder rungs. Happs was so close that Aiden felt Happs's sharp metal edges graze the leather on the sole of Aiden's left boot. He quickly whipped his leg up, whimpering as he did. He couldn't contain the whimper. The image of Jace's disconnected foot filled Aiden with total mind-numbing hysteria.

Aiden was devastated by the death of his friend, of course, but the idea of getting dismembered, for some reason, was one hundred times more horrifying than simply dying. He didn't want to go out the way Jace had. No way.

The ladder pipe was a short one. Aiden didn't think it took him up a full level. Maybe a half level. The ladder pipe came to an end at a fork between two pipes. Again, however, one of the paths was blocked. Once more, Aiden had just one choice.

Glancing down to be sure Happs was stopped at the bottom of the ladder, Aiden started to duck into the open pipe.

He hesitated when he saw that Happs was looking up at him.

Happs had his round white head tipped back, and his one functioning eye was gazing at Aiden intensely. The intent, Aiden thought, looked decidedly evil. But of course, that was crazy. As he'd told Jace, Happs wasn't capable of evil. He was just a robot with a job to do, and he was doing his job the best he could. He didn't care that the results of his efforts were carving up innocent kids. Did he?

Aiden shook his head, but he couldn't tear his gaze from Happs. As Aiden watched, Happs tipped his head back into its usual position and powered backward away from the ladder. Happs turned and slipped back into the ball pit. His butchered treads belching plastic balls up around him, Happs mowed right over the top of Jace's limp, lacerated body and disappeared from Aiden's view.

"He's going to find a way to get to me," Aiden said.

As soon as he spoke, Aiden realized no one was there to hear him. Jace was gone. Didn't Aiden get that? He'd just watched the murdering robot run over the top of his dead friend. Aiden was alone. He was talking to himself.

Aiden had no idea where he was going as he crawled through the pipe. He and Jace had looked for a way out and hadn't found one. What could Aiden do?

He didn't know, but he knew he wasn't going to sit still and wait for Happs to come and shred him. He put his head down and crawled.

Aiden wasn't sure how long he had crawled before he reached a fork . . . that was no longer a fork. One of the pipe openings in front of Aiden was blocked. The other was a gradual slide that curved out of sight.

Aiden looked back over his shoulder. Should he retrace his steps and make his way back to the ball pit? If Happs was looking for him, Happs was no longer in the pit, and maybe the robot wouldn't have the reasoning capacity to return to the place Aiden had fled.

There was only one problem with that idea. Aiden didn't want to return to the ball pit. Jace was in the ball pit. And Jace's blood was in the ball pit.

No, Aiden couldn't face going back to the ball pit. That left him with just one choice. He eased himself feet-first into the gradual slide.

Because he didn't know where Happs was—for all Aiden knew the robot might have been waiting at the bottom of the slide—Aiden was in no hurry to get to the bottom of the pipe. So, he let himself slip slowly downward, trying to ignore the way his imagination conjured up an image of Happs waiting at the bottom.

The pipe Aiden was in, like so many others in this section of the maze, was walled by the two-way mirror. Aiden could see through it easily, but he knew no one could see him.

The slide passed by the back of the laser tag arena, and Aiden watched a couple boys creep around a fake boulder and ambush a couple girls. With their goggles on, the teens weren't easily recognizable, but Aiden was pretty sure they were in his science class. They weren't friends, but he knew them.

If only he'd managed to make more friends. Maybe if he and Jace hadn't been their own universe, guys like Landon wouldn't have picked on them. And if guys like Landon had left them alone, Aiden wouldn't have gotten a black eye. If he hadn't gotten a black eye, maybe he wouldn't have wanted to escape into the maze. Maybe his whole life would have been different. Maybe Jace would still have a life.

Aiden reached the bottom of the gradual slide, and . . . he immediately cursed his vivid imagination. It had turned Aiden's fears into reality.

Happs was coming along the pipe toward the ball pit at the bottom of the slide. He was just twenty feet from the pit.

Swallowing a scream of terror, Aiden scrambled through the balls and crawled into the closest pipe. He clambered as fast as he could through the tube, trying to put as much distance as he could between himself and the pursuing robot.

Happs's chirring sounds echoed behind Aiden. Its chant reverberated through Aiden's chest.

"Out. With me," Happs insisted.

Aiden took a left turn and found himself in a climbing pipe. Nearly leaping up its sides, he grabbed for a handhold, and he pulled himself upward. Below him, Happs clattered closer.

Risking a downward glance, Aiden nearly lost his grip on the pipe when he saw Happs's one working eye look up at him.

Happs began to ascend the pipe like a demented spider. Aiden climbed faster.

At the top of the climbing wall, Aiden faced a junction of three pipes. He didn't stop to think about which way to go. He just crawled down the closest pipe, the one to the right.

The scraping sounds behind Aiden told him that Happs wasn't far behind.

Aiden's knees were screaming at him as he pounded

through the pipe. It was getting harder and harder to move quickly. It felt like the skin over his kneecaps was raw.

He was having trouble breathing, too.

Concentrating on fleeing Happs, Aiden hadn't noticed until now the tears that had been cascading down his cheeks since Jace had died. Now his nose was plugged up from all the crying. He was gasping for air through his mouth. He could hear himself mewling and panting.

And worse, he could hear Happs. The robot continued his chant. "Out. With me."

The chant was way too close.

But the chant wasn't the worst of the sounds trailing after Aiden. The truly appalling sounds were the nails-on-a-blackboard rasps of Happs's jagged metal edges gouging the sides of the pipe behind Aiden. He could all too clearly imagine what he'd feel if Happs reached him.

Almost near the end of the pipe he was in, Aiden spotted a sloping pipe. Although he was tempted to use it, he was pretty sure Happs could easily catch up to him on a slide. So, he kept going, and he discovered this pipe ended up looping back around to the one he'd just been in . . . almost. Just before Aiden reached the juncture of the two pipes, he realized that the pipe he'd just been in was now closed off. Obviously, Happs had damaged it enough to activate another safety barrier.

Aiden glanced over his shoulder and yelped. Happs was only about fifteen feet away.

"Out. With me," Happs said. The blood-stained metal of his killing arms reached for Aiden.

Aiden had no choice now. He was nearly cornered.

He quickly backtracked a couple feet and dove headfirst down the sliding pipe.

The second Aiden landed in the ball pit at the base of the slide, he didn't make the same mistake Jace had made. Aiden didn't try to swim through the pit. Instead, he immediately found his footing and turned to face the slide he'd just come down.

He made the turn barely in time.

Happs came catapulting off the end of the slide the second Aiden faced it. Because Aiden could see Happs's trajectory, though, he was able to fling himself out of the robot's path.

When Happs hit the ball pit, he landed on his head. Aiden knew the robot would right himself quickly, but it would take a few seconds.

Aiden used every one of those seconds to his advantage. Coiling into a tight spring, Aiden launched himself across the ball pit, reaching for the end of the nearest open pipe. He was in the pipe and crawling for all he was worth before he heard Happs's whirring treads thump into the pipe behind him.

Aiden was no longer aware of his body, he realized. He couldn't feel his knees anymore. He couldn't hear his breathing. It was as if his consciousness had transcended his physicality. He was no longer a boy crawling through a maze. He had a single-minded goal: get away from Happs.

Aiden crawled around a bend and let himself, for an instant, feel the relief of having Happs out of his sight. But when he looked at the way ahead, he was dismayed to see that more safety barriers had gone up. He was at a junction, but he only had one choice. Two of the pipes were closed off.

Aiden crawled into the one available pipe.

As soon as Aiden entered the pipe, he recognized it. He and Jace had been in this pipe twice, and Aiden knew it was a loop with only a couple offshoots. He had to get to one of the offshoots before Happs got too close.

Taking a quick glance over his shoulder, Aiden realized that his goal was easier set than accomplished. Happs was the closest he'd ever been. He was less than ten feet away.

Aiden put on the afterburners. He crawled faster than he'd ever crawled in his life.

He crawled so fast that by the time he approached the first offshoot, he'd managed to get about twenty feet ahead of the relentless robot. He charged toward the off-shoot with the first hope he'd felt since Jace had died.

If Aiden remembered right, this offshoot led to a lad-der. Happs couldn't manage ladders. If Aiden could reach the ladder, he could—

Aiden came to an abrupt stop. He'd reached the first offshoot, and it was closed off. A safety partition barred the way.

"No," Aiden whispered.

"Out. With me," Happs said.

He was once again way too close.

Aiden started crawling once more. The other offshoot was just around the curve up ahead. It didn't lead to a ladder, but it did lead to a long tunnel that had a lot of intersecting pipes. Reaching that offshoot would at least give Aiden some options.

If Happs had been a living, breathing creature, Aiden was sure he'd have been able to feel Happs's breath behind him. As it was, Aiden kept expecting to feel Happs's jagged metal appendages slice into his foot at any moment.

For some reason, Aiden was back in his body again. The muscles in his legs were knotted, and his feet felt weird, as if they were curling up in dread of Happs's savage limbs.

Aiden tried to ignore everything he felt. He knew that if he thought about what would happen if Happs reached him, he wouldn't have the strength to keep crawling. And he had to reach the other offshoot.

Just as his body's sensations had returned, Aiden's auditory systems came back online, too. He could once again hear his heaving breath. He could also hear the rhythmic thudding of his knees against the pipe's plastic. And of course, he could hear Happs's clicks and whirrs and grinds and resolute chant getting closer and closer.

Just a few more seconds, Aiden thought. The offshoot was right around the corner.

But it wasn't.

When Aiden sped toward where he expected the offshoot to be, his heart plummeted into his gut.

The offshoot wasn't open anymore. Like the other one, it was now covered by a safety barrier.

Aiden was trapped. And Happs was getting closer.

"Out. With me," Happs ordered him. The robot's

crackly voice was way too loud, which meant it was way too close.

Aiden didn't look back to see just how close Happs was. He didn't want to know.

Given no other choice, Aiden tore past the blocked offshoot. It was instinct to keep going. But Aiden knew his flight from Happs was futile now.

With the offshoots blocked, Aiden was now caught in a closed-off loop. All he could do was go around and around in a circle.

Happs's calamitous pursuit had been activating security barriers all along. Aiden had been essentially herded like an animal into a killing zone. He had nowhere to go. But still, he kept crawling.

As Aiden crawled, he didn't allow himself to think anymore. If he thought, he'd have to ask himself the questions he didn't want to ask:

How long could he stay ahead of Happs? How long would it be before Happs's out-of-control passage through the looped pipe would damage it enough to partition it off even more? How long would it be before Aiden died the same way Jace had?

As Aiden crawled through the pipe, he couldn't help but see the kids beyond the pipe's plastic walls, and he realized he had gotten his wish. He was invisible.

B-7

SITTING ON THE BLUE BRAIDED RUG, CROSS-LEGGED WITH HIS BACK AGAINST THE BIG GRAY SOFA IN HIS FAMILY'S LIVING ROOM, BILLY SNATCHED AN OAT-MEAL COOKIE FROM THE PLATE HIS MOM HAD SET ON THE LOW COFFEE TABLE IN FRONT OF HIM. HE TOOK A BITE AND LOOKED EAGERLY ACROSS THE ROOM TO THE TV.

"It's almost time!" he shouted, spewing cookie crumbs over his skinny, bare legs.

"Don't talk with your mouth full," Billy's father said.

Billy grinned up at his dad. "Sorry," he said, spraying more crumbs. He giggled when he realized what he'd done.

His dad shook his head and ruffled Billy's hair. Then Billy's dad took a seat on the sofa next to Billy's mom. He picked up the newspaper and opened it wide. The paper crackled, and Billy's dad cleared his throat like he always did when he started to read the paper.

Outside, the neighbor's dog barked. That meant it was getting dark. The dog always barked when it started to get dark.

Billy liked these "always" things. He was only five years old, but he'd already learned that the world could be a scary place. When he was three, he got really sick, and he had to have lots of awful needles stuck in his back, and he had to be away from his parents. It was terrifying, and he never knew when something like that would happen again. Always things felt like they kept bad surprises away. When always things happened, Billy could tell himself everything was okay.

Billy's mom reached out and turned on the big blue lamp sitting on the end table next to her. The lamp filled the room with yellowish light. She nudged Billy's dad.

"You know, if you set a better example," Billy's mom said, "he wouldn't do that."

"Hmm," Billy's dad said. He always said "hmm" if you talked to him while he read the paper.

Billy wasn't sure what his mom meant about a better example, but he didn't care much. All he cared about right now was that *Freddy and Friends* was about to start.

"Like father like son," Billy's mom went on.

Out of the corner of his eye, Billy saw his mom elbow his dad.

"You always talk with your mouth full at dinner when you get revved up about work," Billy's mom said. "You two are like peas in a pod."

Billy did know what that meant. His mom had said that a lot of times, most recently on Billy's fifth birthday.

"You look and act more and more like your father every year," his mom had said to Billy the morning of his birthday. She'd been helping him get dressed, and she'd been looking over his head into the full-length mirror on the back of his bedroom door. "You're like two peas in a pod."

Gazing at his reflection, Billy had seen what his mom meant . . . sort of. With brown hair that never wanted to lay down quite right, small brown eyes, a round nose and cheeks, and a wide mouth, Billy did look like a shrunk-down version of his dad. He didn't look at all like his pretty blonde mom. He just looked like his dad. He didn't really think he acted like his dad, though. His dad wasn't home that much. He went to an office and worked all the time. And when he was home, he was usually either reading the paper, watching sports on TV, or sleeping.

Billy did a lot more stuff than his dad did. He thought the only thing they had in common was TV, and they watched different stuff. For instance, his dad never wanted to watch *Freddy and Friends*.

Billy gazed at the TV and when the Fazbear Entertainment logo filled the screen, he bounced up and down on his butt. "It's starting!" he squealed.

"We're switching to the game in fifteen minutes," Billy's dad said.

Billy's mom picked up a magazine and started flipping through it. "Oh, good grief, Dan," she said. "Let him watch his show. You can miss fifteen minutes of your precious game."

Billy's dad said something in response, but Billy didn't hear his dad's words. Billy was too busy watching Freddy, Chica, and Bonnie eat pizza and talk about the camera on the wall above them.

"Who do you think is watching us?" a cartoon Bonnie on the TV asked.

"I don't know, Bonnie," cartoon Freddy said.

"Let's go see if we can find whoever it is," cartoon Chica said.

On the TV screen, Bonnie jumped up and grabbed his guitar. "Not until after we play a song," he said.

"Okay," Freddy said. He pulled out a mic and started singing.

Billy watched, fascinated.

Billy liked all the animatronics, but Freddy was his favorite. Freddy was brown, like Billy's hair, and Freddy was the one in charge. Billy liked the idea of being in charge. He liked the idea of being a big animatronic, too. Animatronics were robots. They were strong, and he knew they didn't feel bad things like real people did. It would be nice not to feel bad things.

A commercial for Freddy Fazbear's Pizzeria came on the screen. It showed one of the real animatronics in the middle of a performance.

Billy grabbed the TV remote and jumped to his feet. Pretending the remote was a microphone, he started dancing and singing at the top of his lungs.

Billy's mom laughed. She put down her magazine and clapped her hands. Billy's dad lowered his paper and watched Billy perform.

"I'm an animatronic!" Billy shouted.

Billy's mom and dad smiled and nodded. "Okay, Billy," they said in unison, "you're an animatronic."

Billy began marching, stiff-legged, around the living room. He stomped hard as he walked, rattling the lamps on the end tables and all his mom's knickknacks.

Billy plodded over to the entryway, right off the living room. He yanked coats off the coatrack and grabbed the rack, pretending it was a microphone stand. Pulling the stand over, he bent at the waist and sang into it.

On the TV, the show returned to the screen. Billy dropped the coatrack and trudged back over to the coffee table, pretending to be like Freddy the whole time. He sat back down on the floor again, but he did it as if his arms and legs were made of metal like the animatronics' arms and legs. He put his legs straight out in front of him instead of crossing them. He liked how it felt to move like that. It made him feel big and powerful. It made him feel like nothing could hurt him.

The next morning, Billy stomped down the stairs to the kitchen. He was still being an animatronic. He liked being an animatronic.

Keeping his back very straight, Billy sat at the round

table in his mom's yellow-and-white kitchen. Morning sun peeked past girly flowered curtains covering the big windows by the table.

Billy looked outside. In a loud voice as robotic as he could make it, he said, "It is a pretty day. I want to go to the park after school."

Billy's dad walked into the room. "Why are you shouting?" he asked Billy.

"I am not shouting," Billy said loudly. "I am a robot, and this is how I talk."

"Oh," Billy's dad said. "Okay."

Billy saw his dad raise his eyebrow at his mom. She made a fluttery gesture with her hand. Billy's dad sighed.

Taking the chair next to Billy's, Billy's dad accepted the cup of coffee Billy's mom handed to him. Billy's dad took a sip, then sat up really straight and said, "Oh no, I think the coffee has fried my circuits." He made a bunch of sputtering noises that sounded like a radio between stations. He went stiff and then let his head fall forward to the table with a thunk.

Billy laughed a robotic ha-ha-ha. He poked his dad's shoulder.

"You need to go to Parts and Service so you can be repaired," Billy said in his new robot voice. "I will save your chair while you are gone."

Billy's dad raised his head. "That is a good idea," he said in a deep booming voice. "I will go to Parts and Service."

Billy's dad got up and stepped over to Billy's mom. "I'll take my coffee to go and pick up something at work," he whispered to her.

She nodded and poured his coffee into a travel mug.

"How long do you think he's going to be an animatronic?" Billy's dad asked, still whispering.

Billy's mom smiled over at Billy. He gave her a big smile back, exposing his teeth the way animatronics did.

"He'll get bored with it soon enough," Billy's mom whispered.

Billy wondered why they were whispering. He could hear everything they said. Animatronics had very good auditory sensors. And they didn't get bored easily.

When Billy's mom took him to his kindergarten class after breakfast, Billy marched into the bright, colorful room filled with playing kids, and he announced, "I am an animatronic." He pretended he was made of metal as he walked over to his friends.

Two of Billy's friends immediately started acting like robots, too. Clark, small and redheaded, made a good robot. He walked with his arms straight out in front of him, and he spoke with a mechanical voice. Peter wasn't as good at being a robot because he moved too fast and bent too much. But he, too, did a pretty good robotic voice. "Robots will take over the world," he announced.

"Robots rule!" Billy agreed.

Billy's friend Sadie didn't like that Billy was a robot. She tossed her black pigtails, put her hands on her hips, and said, "You're not a robot, Billy. You're being dumb."

Billy stomped over to Sadie and pushed her. "I am a robot, and you cannot call me dumb."

Sadie ran to their teacher, Mrs. Foswick. Mrs. Foswick,

who was very tall and had short hair and could have been a good animatronic herself, put Billy in a time-out. It wasn't a real time-out, though, because she didn't turn him off, and as long as an animatronic wasn't turned off, it kept going.

So, Billy sat in the corner of the kindergarten class-room, and he sang. No matter what Mrs. Foswick said to him, he didn't stop singing. Mrs. Foswick got very upset. Billy didn't tell her that all she had to do was switch him off because he didn't want to be switched off.

Billy didn't tell his mom that he could be switched off, either, when she came to pick him up early. All he did was stand tall and straight while his mom talked to Mrs. Foswick, and then he left the school with his mom, marching to the family station wagon and getting in the back seat. There, he sat bold upright, his head swiveling left and right as his visual sensors gathered data about his surroundings and stored it in his processor, which then told him that the sun had gone behind clouds, and it was raining. Billy was glad he was inside the car. Rain wasn't good for animatronics.

When Billy's mom got behind the wheel of the car, she turned to look at Billy. "You made Mrs. Foswick unhappy," she said.

"Mrs. Foswick does not like singing robots," Billy told her.

Billy's mom smiled at Billy. "That might be true. But I like singing robots. What do you want to sing on the way home?"

Billy thought about it. "I think we should sing a

round." He began singing, "Row, row, row your boat." As soon as he reached, "Gently down the stream," his mom joined in.

Billy thought it was good that his mom liked singing robots.

After Billy and his mom went through the song twice, his mom asked, "What do singing robots like to eat for lunch?"

"Pizza!" Billy boomed.

"Pizza it is," Billy's mom said. She glanced at Billy in her rearview mirror as she turned the car in the direction of Freddy Fazbear's Pizzeria.

Billy's circuits returned to processing his surroundings. They took note of the passing cars, the birds hopping around under bushes near the road, and the rows of houses along the sidewalk. They filed everything in Billy's memory banks so that when Billy's dad came home from work that night, Billy was able to recite the afternoon's events perfectly.

At first, Billy's dad seemed surprised by the list of things Billy's processors recorded that day, but then he smiled and said, "Well, let's see what my processors recorded today." He then listed all the things he had seen since he left the house that morning. It turned out he hadn't seen much. Billy's dad spent the day in his small office. It didn't take him long to list his desk, his shelves, his computer, his window looking out at a parking lot, and the pictures of Billy and Billy's mom that hung on the wall.

When Billy's mom put salad and chicken on the table

in front of Billy and his dad, Billy said, "Robots do not eat salad."

"Some do," Billy's dad said. "It depends on their settings." Billy's dad reached out and turned a switch under Billy's ear. "There, now you're a robot that eats salads."

Billy checked with his internal systems to see if this was true. Apparently, it was, but his systems didn't say Billy had to like the salad. So, he ate it, and he didn't like it.

The next day, Mrs. Foswick was much nicer to Billy. When he stomped into the classroom, Mrs. Foswick rushed up to Billy and said, "Hi, Billy. Come with me."

Mrs. Foswick took Billy's hand. He let her close her fingers over his stiff ones. Bending his arm only slightly, he walked with her, lifting his feet and bringing them down hard on the room's purple-and-blue rubber flooring.

"I made a special place for you," Mrs. Foswick said. "It's a place just for animatronics,"

Mrs. Foswick led Billy to the back of the classroom, and she sat him at a desk. A big cardboard sign on the desk had a drawing of a robot connected by a cord to a chair. Under the drawing, big black letters stretched across the sign.

"Do you know what letter that is?" Mrs. Foswick asked Billy, pointing at the first one.

Billy recognized it. "That is an *A*," Billy said.

"That's right!" Mrs. Foswick said. "What a smart robot you are!"

Mrs. Foswick motioned to her teacher's assistant, Miss Harper. She was the opposite of Mrs. Foswick; Miss Harper was short and had long hair that she wore in a ponytail. She was very nice. Miss Harper came over and smiled at Billy. She pulled up a chair and sat next to him.

"Miss Harper is going to, um, program your circuits with more letters so you can read this sign by the end of the day," Mrs. Foswick said. "Does that sound good, Billy?"

Billy nodded stiffly several times. It was good for animatronics to learn new things.

Billy started singing about learning new things. He sang everything that Miss Harper taught him.

While Miss Harper taught Billy, the other kids learned and played like normal. Billy's friends, Clark and Peter, had stopped being animatronics. Instead, they'd started laughing at Billy. So had the other kids. They said it was stupid that he was still acting like a robot.

Billy didn't care about what the other kids said, because animatronics didn't care about things like that. He ignored the other kids, and he put his attention only on Miss Harper and what she was uploading to his data banks.

By the end of the day, Billy knew what the word *animatronics* looked like in letters. And he knew the sign on the desk said, ANIMATRONIC CHARGING STATION.

"This will be your place in this classroom for as long as you're an animatronic," Miss Harper told Billy.

"I'll always be an animatronic," Billy sang.

★ ★ ★

That night, Billy lay on his back in bed. He refused his mom's offer to "curl up with Max." First, animatronics didn't curl up. Second, they didn't have stuffed teddy bears named Max. Billy lay straight and stiff, his arms at his sides.

Animatronics didn't sleep, either, but they could act like humans. Billy closed his eyes. He knew that, soon, he would be turned off so his circuits could reboot.

His mom bent over and kissed his forehead. She sighed. "Good night, Billy," she said.

"Good night, Mom," Billy said.

Billy listened to his mom's footsteps shuffle across his thick red carpet. Even through his closed eyes, his visual sensors picked up on the room's light going out. Then his auditory sensors zeroed in on his mom's voice. She was standing in his bedroom doorway.

"I'm not sure what else we can do at this point," she whispered. "I talked to Mrs. Foswick, and she agreed to play along. She assigned Miss Harper to work with Billy separately from the other kids."

"This is going on for too long," Billy's dad said.

"It's only been a couple days," Billy's mom responded. "Let's give it some time. He'll get tired of it soon."

Billy's processors tried to compute what he might get tired of. He was experiencing being tired in general right now. His programming was very good; he knew he should be tired when he had to go to bed. He was a very good animatronic.

As he listened to his parents talking, Billy's programming began to update. The update was a download of information related to being a little boy. Billy was an animatronic, yes, but he was an animatronic designed to be his parents' son. To be his parents' son, he had to act like a small child who went to kindergarten and played games.

Billy wasn't just a good animatronic; he was also a top-of-the-line animatronic. This meant he could perform any tasks set by his programming. He could act like a child and play games. He could do it well.

The next morning, Billy stiffly began following his new programming. Although he was still limited by his metal limbs and he could only speak in whole words because that was what his voice box allowed, he started being his parents' son and being a little kid in kindergarten instead of being a singing robot.

This new version of Billy the animatronic seemed to make everyone a little happier. Although Billy's friends still made fun of him, Mrs. Foswick, Miss Harper, and Billy's parents seemed pleased with the improved version of the Billy animatronic . . . at least for a while.

As an animatronic, Billy wasn't aware of the passage of time. He didn't keep track of days and weeks and months. He did note, however, when his mom stopped taking him to the kindergarten classroom.

"Have my operating specs changed again?" Billy asked the first morning his mom didn't put him in the car to take him to school.

Billy's mom, who was making pancakes, turned and frowned at Billy. "What?"

"You did not take me to school," Billy said.

Billy's mom frowned again. Then she quickly replaced the frown with a smile. Sometimes her expressions would change fast like that, and Billy would wonder if his mom was an animatronic, too.

"School's out for the summer, Billy," his mom said.

Billy ran this through his circuits. He discovered his programming needed another update.

"What does a Billy animatronic do when it is not in school?" Billy asked.

"Fun things," his mom answered.

"I will need you to input a list of those things so I can operate right," Billy told her.

His mom put a plate of pancakes in front of Billy. "Start with eating pancakes. That's fun."

Billy lifted his fork and cut into the pancakes. He acted like it was fun.

Vera pulled on her green cotton nightshirt and watched her husband, wearing his favorite baggy pj's, pull back the covers and get into their king-size bed. He switched on the brass lamp that sat on his nightstand.

Dan looked at Vera. "We have to do something about Billy."

Vera turned back the covers on her side of the bed. She got under the sheets and leaned against her plumped-up pillows. She didn't answer Dan at first. She just surveyed their lovely bedroom. Decorated in neutral beige and brown tones, their bedroom was a calm oasis from the stresses of everyday life. She'd decorated the room herself, and she took pride in how comfortable and soothing it was.

It wasn't soothing her tonight, though.

"I know we have to do something," Vera finally said.

Oh, how she knew. It had been over six months since her sweet little boy had stopped being her sweet little boy and instead had started acting like an animatronic.

Dan picked up the TV remote, but he didn't turn on the TV. "If I'd known that show would have this effect on him," Dan said, "I'd never have allowed him to watch it."

"How were we supposed to know?" Vera asked. "It's just a silly little show."

"I have half a mind to sue Fazbear Entertainment," Dan said.

Vera turned and glared at Dan. "And how would that help Billy?" she asked. "It doesn't matter who's responsible. What matters is taking care of him."

"Why can't he like sports like a normal little boy?" Dan asked.

Vera slapped his arm. "Every child is different. I keep telling you that. Not all boys like sports."

Dan sighed. He toyed with the remote. "And you're still sure that going along with all this is the right idea?" Dan asked.

Vera shrugged. "I called Dr. Lingstrom this morning after Billy asked me to 'input' a list of fun things."

"I'm not sure I have much faith in Dr. Lingstrom," Dan said. "She's been seeing Billy for four months, and it's not helping."

"I don't think child psychology is a precise science," Vera said. "But she assured me again that this kind of make-believe is perfectly natural for a kid Billy's age."

"I bet she's never heard of a kid walking and talking like a robot all the time for over six months!" Dan protested.

Vera chewed on her lower lip. "Well, no. But she said she did treat a kid who pretended to be an alien for over a year."

"Why did he stop?" Dan asked.

"Dr. Lingstrom wasn't sure. He just started acting normally again one day." Vera reached out for a tube of lotion. She slathered some on her hands, inhaling the lotion's soothing lavender fragrance.

In the last few months, Vera had done a lot of research on how to ease anxiety. Lavender was supposed to be relaxing. She now used lavender-scented shampoo, conditioner, and lotion, and she'd put lavender sachets in every drawer and closet in their bedroom. Dan had started complaining about it. Apparently, his clothes smelled so much like lavender that his coworkers had started teasing him about it.

"I wish Billy would go back to normal," Dan said.

"Me too," Vera said.

Billy found he was very good at meeting the "fun" protocol of his new programming. It mostly required him to play with toys in his yard and sit in front of the TV. It also included going to the park, eating ice cream, and playing games with his mom. It didn't, Billy noticed, involve spending time with friends. Billy didn't have friends anymore. Apparently, other kids didn't like animatronics.

In addition to his fun tasks, Billy was required to visit

Dr. Lingstrom. This had been something he was expected to do for several months. It had started while he was still being Billy in kindergarten.

Dr. Lingstrom, Billy's sensors told him, was a young woman with big glasses and a bun on the top of her head. Billy always saw her in a pale blue office that held a desk and a play area filled with blocks and dolls. Dr. Lingstrom had Billy sit in the play area, and she told him to play with the blocks and dolls. Billy, already programmed for fun, didn't have trouble with the play. He only had trouble when Dr. Lingstrom asked questions like "Why do you think you're an animatronic?" and "Do you remember being just a little boy?"

These questions were very challenging for Billy's chips to process. They made no sense.

Billy always answered the questions the same. "I think I am an animatronic because I am an animatronic," Billy said. "I have never been just a little boy. I am programmed to act like one, and I do that."

Dr. Lingstrom asked Billy a lot of questions that required him to access his memory banks. He answered them all. He had a lot of images and information in his memory banks.

Nothing Billy said, though, seemed to make Dr. Lingstrom happy. Billy had trouble making sense of these visits with the serious woman. They were not consistent with his function of "fun." The two things didn't seem to go together.

Mostly, though, Billy's "fun" programming was effective. One day, though, the fun protocol ended. Billy's mom took him to another classroom. This was first grade, she said, and it was in a new school, a "private" school. None of Billy's old friends were in this school, his mom said. She said he could make new friends. Billy thought she was wrong. He didn't think these kids would like animatronics any more than his old friends did.

When Billy's mom told him about the new school, Billy told her he needed a new download. What tasks would he be expected to perform? She told him to go to the classroom and learn.

On the first day of first grade, Billy's new teacher, a curly-haired woman named Mrs. Cromwell, asked the children to stand up and introduce themselves. "Tell us your name and what you like to do," she said.

Billy's auditory systems processed as three children stood and did as they'd been instructed.

"I'm Elly," a little blonde girl said. "I like to dance."

"I'm Vick," a dark-skinned boy said. "I like baseball."

"I'm Terry," a short boy said, "I play chess."

Mrs. Cromwell pointed at Billy. Billy unfolded his metal limbs. He stood bolt upright, his arms straight at his sides. "I am an animatronic named Billy," he said. "I like doing what I am programmed to do."

The other kids in the room started laughing. Mrs. Cromwell stood. "Shush! Everyone hush. Be nice."

The laughter died down to a few giggles and snorts. Billy was not bothered by the sounds. He was an animatronic. He didn't have feelings. Nothing bothered him.

According to Billy's mom, the new private school had a lot of classes that normal schools didn't have. Billy's mom told him this when she was updating his servers before he went to bed. She called this process "tucking him in." It was the time when she gave him the information that he required to do what he needed to do the next day.

"They even have a beginning robotics class for first graders," Billy's mom said. "You'll learn how robots work."

Billy knew how robots worked. He was a robot. He knew how he worked.

The next day, however, Billy discovered that the class did teach him something. Robots, he learned, needed a special oil to lubricate their joints. Billy had never been oiled. He filed away the information in his data banks. He would do something about it when he was returned home after school.

For a period of time—Billy wasn't sure how long a time—Billy followed the protocol for a well-oiled robot. He found the necessary oil in the garage, on his dad's workbench. The oil was clear and thick. It didn't register as "pleasant" to Billy's taste sensors, and it gave him sensations that were not his usual state—aches in his middle and in his head—but he didn't let that keep him from properly caring for his parts.

At meals, Billy ate less and less food. In the garage, he took in more and more oil.

One day, though, Billy's systems malfunctioned. When he tried to raise himself out of bed in the morning, he immediately registered that something was wrong.

In his animatronic belly, pressing pain-like sensory

input constricted Billy's internal parts. Aware that small beads of water had appeared on his forehead, Billy had to concentrate to get his mechanical body to make the trek from his room to the kitchen. Instead of feeling strong like he usually did, he felt like he was going to fall over. He almost didn't make it to his chair in the kitchen.

Concentrating on putting eggs and sausage on a plate, Billy's mom didn't notice that he was malfunctioning. She didn't notice, that is, until after Billy had consumed—as he'd been programmed to—the entire plateful of eggs and sausage. It was at that point that the smell of the sausage glitched up Billy's olfactory sensors, causing the sensors to trigger a cascade of system failures. Billy's stomach parts and his throat parts crashed together, and the eggs and sausage came back up. They erupted from his open mouth and splashed all over the floor.

That day, Billy's mom took him to Parts and Service . . . although, she called Parts and Service "the hospital." Billy's memory banks brought up images of him being in "the hospital" when he was three, but the images did not have any negative impact on him. He was a robot, so he couldn't be upset by anything. Parts and Service was just another place to be; it was neither good nor bad. Therefore, animatronic Billy was calm while he was given a complete system-wide check. The check determined that he was temporarily out of service, what his mom called "sick."

Billy didn't have to stay in Parts and Service for long, though. When he came home, he reasoned that he was fully reconfigured. He returned to his self-oiling routine. He thought it was a good routine. Maybe it wasn't, though. He was back in Parts and Service again the next day.

In Parts and Service, a round-bellied, bald-headed animatronic repair person (called Dr. Reynolds) was able to detect the oil that Billy had been using. This oil, Dr. Reynolds said, was "a very bad idea."

"But I am an animatronic," Billy objected. "I must keep my joints lubricated."

Dr. Reynolds had a conference with Billy's mom while Billy lay flat on his back in a bed with metal railings on the side. He lay there and looked up at a white ceiling. Dr. Reynolds and Billy's mom whispered, but Billy could hear every word.

"He's in Dr. Lingstrom's care," Billy's mom told Dr. Reynolds.

"And what does she say?" Dr. Reynolds asked.

"She says we should play along with his fantasy. If we don't, it could cause a psychotic break."

Billy ran the words *psychotic break* through his databases. He had no information about the word *psychotic*, but *break* had many meanings. He suspected that some of his systems were damaged in some way. This did not concern him. He trusted that Dr. Reynolds would repair them.

"A psychotic break will be the least of your problems if he keeps ingesting oil," Dr. Reynolds said.

"Well, then," Billy's mom said, "you need to tell him there's another way to oil his joints."

Dr. Reynolds and Billy's mom stopped talking. They walked over to the bed.

"Sit up, Billy," Dr. Reynolds instructed.

Billy sat up.

"You want to keep your systems in good shape, don't you?" Dr. Reynolds said.

"Good animatronics self-regulate," Billy said.

Dr. Reynolds nodded. "Then I need to add some important information to your database. Are you ready for inputting?"

Billy nodded. He directed his unblinking gaze at Dr. Reynolds.

"The best oil for your particular kind of animatronic joints," Dr. Reynolds said, "is olive oil. It's something that your mom can put in your food, and if you eat the food she cooks, your joints will function perfectly."

Billy looked from his mom to Dr. Reynolds and back again. He concentrated on letting the information process. In spite of the whispered conversation that he'd heard—which was something his processor couldn't quite compute—this new data was consistent with Billy's goal of being the best animatronic he could be. Because of this, Billy nodded once. "I will comply."

Billy remained in Parts and Service for another day. Then his mom brought him home.

He returned to being a good animatronic.

Although Billy wasn't able to keep track of time very well, he learned that certain days came just once a year, so when these days came around, he knew a year had gone by. Christmas was one of these special days.

Billy had a whole set of operating protocols for

Christmas. They were protocols similar to summer "fun" protocols, but they were more specific. At Christmastime, Billy was required to help his parents hang strings of white lights on the trees outside and help put bright hanging things on a tree that was brought inside. Billy was also required to unwrap brightly wrapped boxes that were put under the tree. This was a simple task. He opened the boxes, looked at what was inside, said, "Thank you," then put the object aside before opening the next box.

Animatronic Billy had four of these tree-centered days in his memory banks before an event occurred that required him to establish some new neural networks. The event was preceded by a conversation that his auditory sensors recorded as he was passing his parents' closed bedroom door on the way to the bathroom. (Although animatronics generally had no need to pee or do any of the other things done in bathrooms, Billy was nothing if not fully devoted to his child protocol. He was, he believed, a most rare animatronic in that he'd developed the ability to pee and brush his teeth and bathe like a normal child. The fact that all the water involved in bathing didn't short out his circuits or rust his metal endoskeleton was a testament to the effectiveness of ingesting his mom's olive oil.)

Billy usually didn't allow his parents' conversations to use up his RAM, but the night he was heading to the bathroom, he felt compelled—for reasons he didn't understand—to stop and listen. Perhaps it was the word *institution* that had triggered his attention. This was a word unfamiliar to him.

Billy was, however, an animatronic with exceptional artificial intelligence. He could learn, and one of the things he'd learned was that he could often add to his knowledge base by placing new words or experiences in the context of their surroundings. To that end, he listened to his mom and dad talk so he could discern the meaning of *institution*.

"I'm not putting him in an institution," Billy's mom hissed right after Billy's dad spoke. "He's my son. After everything he went through when he was three, when we had to leave him in intensive care . . . No, I'm not leaving him anywhere again. He's staying home with me."

"At what cost, Vera? You've been going along with this insane fantasy for over four years. Four years! It just can't go on."

"I think he'll give it up soon."

Something thudded against the door. Billy's auditory processors told him a shoe had just hit the wood.

"We don't know that!" Billy's dad shouted.

"Shh!" Billy's mom said. "He'll hear you."

"I don't care if he hears me!" Billy's dad yelled. "I don't care about anything anymore. I can't take it, Vera. I can't. We have a freak for a son! And we have no life. We can't go anywhere or do anything with him. All we can do is sit at home and watch our little boy pretend to be a robot. That's not living. That's hell."

Footsteps stomped across the floor behind the door. Billy strode as quickly as his rigid legs allowed into the bathroom. There, he closed the door. He heard his parents' door open. More thudding footsteps. Then silence.

Billy sat on the closed toilet seat and worked through what he'd heard. His dad, it seemed, didn't like animatronics anymore. Oh well, that was okay. Billy didn't need his dad to like him. Billy was still a very good animatronic, whether his dad liked him or not.

Billy's dad left two days after the conversation Billy heard. He left, and he didn't come back.

"Why did Dad leave?" Billy asked as he watched his mom sauté mushrooms and onions in olive oil. She was making spaghetti sauce. This was a red sauce that Billy thought resembled human blood. He wasn't convinced that eating it was appropriate, but he had no data with which to reach a definite conclusion.

Billy's mom, who had been crying off and on throughout the day, wiped a hand across her eyes. She stopped sautéing and came over to the table to sit with Billy. She took Billy's hand.

Billy, as a robot, had no need for physical touch. However, he found that the feel of his mom's hand was agreeable to his tactile sensors. Therefore, he sat stiffly and let her hold his hand.

"Your dad doesn't understand, Billy," Billy's mom said. "He thinks you can make yourself be something besides who you are."

Billy cocked his head, running this through his programming. "It is not possible for a thing to be not the thing it is," he said. "The thing is the thing."

Billy's mom made a sharp laughing sound—one laugh;

it was like the bark of a big sea lion. Billy had seen sea lions on TV. They were part of his animal database, which was quite large.

Billy's mom stood. She patted Billy on the top of the head. "Spoken like a wise little animatronic," she said.

"I am not as little as I was before," Billy said. He saw himself in his mirror every day. He was much bigger than he used to be. He thought he looked even more like his dad now than he used to. But that didn't matter anymore. His dad was gone. Billy just looked like himself, like Billy, the animatronic.

"That's true," Billy's mom said. "And you'll keep getting bigger." She started to return to the stove, then turned back to the table.

"Billy?"

"I am here," Billy answered.

"Have you ever heard of an animatronic growing before?" Billy's mom's eyes were wet and intense. She stared so hard at Billy that, for a moment, she looked like an animatronic, too.

Billy ran the question through his processors. The answer came quickly. "No, I have not heard of a growing animatronic."

"Does that bother you?" Billy's mom asked. Her eyes shone even brighter.

Billy got the idea that his mom wanted him to say something specific. He wasn't able to access information that told him what that was.

"No," Billy said. "I am an animatronic. I do not get

bothered. And why is it important that there are no other animatronics like me? There are many things that exist that I have never heard of. I am unique."

Billy's mom wiped her eyes again. She sighed. "Yes, you are," she said. She returned to the stove and added a can of tomatoes to the mushrooms and onions.

By the time Billy finished what was called sixth grade, he had concluded—based on the totality of his experience observing the humans around him and integrating the information that he read—that he could expand his data banks and upgrade his processors more effectively without the dubious help of "teachers" and "school." Both of these things, he'd discovered, attempted to place restrictions on how Billy took in the world, and the limitations of the restrictions far outweighed any benefit he received from either teachers or school.

Because Billy was an exceptional animatronic, his processors were able to integrate information from multiple sources. One of those sources was books. He was able to upload massive amounts of information from books.

This was why, on the first morning of what would have been Billy's seventh grade, he announced to his mom, "I will not go to school today."

Billy's mom had looked unexpectedly happy about this. She'd rushed over to Billy, where he sat on the edge of his sleeping platform. (The year before, he'd requested that his bed be replaced with a steel table. It was a far better recharging platform for an animatronic.)

"Why don't you want to go to school?" Billy's mom asked. "Are you feeling sick?"

Billy cocked his head and attempted to work out why the idea of him being sick made his mom's eyes light up and her mouth widen into a smile different than the small ones he usually saw on her face. Billy's processors informed him that his mom's expression indicated happiness.

Billy's mom leaned toward him and looked intently into his eyes. "What are you feeling, Billy?" she asked.

"I do not feel," Billy answered. "I am an animatronic."

Billy's mom's smile disappeared. Her eyes moistened, and she rubbed them. Her shoulders slumped.

"I will not go to school," Billy told his mom, "because the disadvantages of school outweigh the advantages. I will add to my databases by reading books. All I will require from you are rides to the library to acquire the books necessary for my continued learning."

Billy's mom gazed at Billy for a long time. He gazed back at her. His visual sensors processed what he saw.

Billy had noted that as he got bigger and his face looked more like that of his now absent dad, his mom got smaller (more accurately, narrower) and her face looked less like her face. Billy had in his memory banks the image of his mom's round and smooth face, her bright blue eyes, and her shiny and bouncy blonde hair. The round face, however, was no longer round. It was more oblong and it revealed the bone structure under his mom's skin. The skin itself didn't seem to fit the bones. It sagged, folding into little pleats between her eyes, around her mouth, and at her jawline. The skin was a different color, too. Before, the skin had been pinkish. Now it looked kind of gray.

Billy's mom's eyes and hair were different, too. Her eyes had lost some of their color; they were now a faded blue. And her hair had no shine. It didn't bounce, either; it hung limply like the kind of hair Billy had seen on a rag doll. (The little girl who lived next door had a rag doll. That little girl didn't like Billy. She once screamed at him that if he got close to her, she'd have her doll eat him up. Billy was unable to process this. From what he knew of dolls, one could not consume him.)

Billy's mom interrupted his internal processing. She patted his thigh and stood. "I'll get your breakfast," she said.

After breakfast, Billy's mom took him to the library. There, he checked out a stack of eight books. This was the largest number of books he was allowed to take out at one time.

"I will be back in two days," Billy informed the large gray-haired librarian when she pushed the stack of books across the counter to him.

The woman nodded several times. Then she ran to the other end of the counter. Billy determined that something had made her nervous. He didn't know what that was.

Billy spent the rest of that first day of no school sitting in the chair at his desk. He read all day until his processors informed him it was time for dinner. When he received that cue, Billy stood and left his room. He started down the hall, heading toward the kitchen.

As Billy walked in his usual stiff-armed and stiff-legged way, he accessed a memory of how he had walked when he'd first become an animatronic. He had strode with too much force, so that every step he took stomped on the ground and rattled everything in the room he was in. It was Dr. Lingstrom who had updated Billy's systems, programming him for a quieter way of getting around.

"You see," she'd told him when she'd demonstrated the new way he was to move, "you can move your metal arms and legs without putting your feet down with so much force." She walked across the room using a gait similar to Billy's. Billy noted how she placed her feet so that her footfalls were silent and didn't make anything shake.

Billy had mimicked Dr. Lingstrom and found the result satisfactory. He had walked quietly ever since.

So, now Billy approached the kitchen silently. He could hear his mom moving around in the small room, but she couldn't hear him.

As Billy got to the doorway, before he stepped into his mom's view, he discerned that she was talking. Because he knew no one was in the house besides him and his mom, Billy deduced she was talking on the phone.

Billy liked the phone. He had discovered that communicating via the phone was usually more affective. It did away with the complexity of processing multiple sensory cues at once. The phone required only auditory processing.

Because listening to his mom's phone conversations often resulted in updating Billy's systems (she said things to other people that she didn't say to him), he stopped just outside the doorway to the kitchen. He focused on his mom's words.

"I just don't know what to do now," Billy's mom said. "You told me not to force him into anything, so I didn't make him go to school. But without other kids to emulate, how will he learn to be a normal boy?"

Billy ran this question through his neural networks. Did it mean that he was not effectively performing his function as his mom's son?

Billy listened more. Perhaps the conversation would give him more information to add to his systems.

"No, no, I told you I'm not putting him someplace. You said as long as he wasn't a danger to himself or anyone else, I could keep him at home."

Billy knew he was not dangerous to anyone. Although robots could be programmed to be destructive, Billy wasn't one of those. He was designed to value human life.

"Yes, I can take care of him," his mom said. "He's my son. You know I work from home, so I can be here for him every day. I'll do whatever he needs."

Working from home was a concept Billy understood. His mom had inputted all the necessary information about that. She was, she told him, a financial advisor and investor. She managed people's money, and she also invested her own money. She did this on her computer in the office next to her bedroom. After his mom introduced Billy to the concept of investing, he checked out books on the subject. The librarian had told him the books were "too old" for him. This was not something Billy could process, so he ignored it. He read the books.

He wasn't able to integrate all the information into his systems, but he stored much of it, and he continued to add to that knowledge base.

"Every child is different," Billy's mom was saying into the phone now. "Billy is Billy. I'm not going to force him to see himself differently than he does, even if what he sees isn't normal."

Billy was an animatronic, so he didn't feel. But when his mom spoke, he experienced a sensation that might have been similar to an emotion. He felt an unusual warmth in the area of his heart. His processors prompted him to step into the kitchen and approach his mom.

When Billy's mom saw Billy, she quickly said good-bye and hung up the phone. Billy walked over to her and rigidly encircled her sticklike shoulders with his own strong arms.

Billy's mom widened her eyes at him. Then she put her arms around him. And she cried.

One of the special days that gave Billy the ability to mark the passing of years was his "birthday." A birthday, Billy understood, was the day that a human was born into the world.

Because Billy was an animatronic, his birthday was more aptly called his "creation day." He informed his mom of this fact the third year of his animatronic existence. Billy's dad was still living with Billy and his mom then, and his dad said "creation day" was absurd. Billy's mom said it was very clever, and from that point on, Billy had creation days.

The number of Billy's accumulated creation days was the subject of debate between Billy and his mom. She thought he was created five years before the number of years Billy had tallied. She told him that he'd started as a baby and lived for five years before he became an animatronic. Billy was able to find these years in his memory banks, but the images he had of those years were distorted, as if they belonged in some other animatronic. He concluded, after devoting much of his RAM to this issue, that the five years to which his mom referred were years during which Billy was being constructed. Given that his memory informed him he was complete on the day he watched Freddy and Friends and announced his existence as an animatronic, Billy believed his creation day was that day, not five years before. When he related this reasoning to his mom, she had nodded and said, "We have to agree to disagree."

Therefore, on Billy's thirteenth creation day, his mom celebrated his eighteenth creation day.

From the human perspective, the eighteenth creation day was a milestone. Accordingly, Billy's mom performed an elaborate celebratory ritual that included a HAPPY CREATION DAY banner, eighteen silver helium balloons, a variety of foods that fit Billy's animatronic dietary requirements, and a large cake (white with white frosting, per those animatronic requirements). Billy, his mom, and Dr. Lingstrom were the only participants in the ritual. They wore silver party hats (specially printed with the words HAPPY CREATION DAY), and they sat at the kitchen table eating the creation day meal.

Billy, of course, acted no differently than usual. He never did. He was an animatronic. He didn't get excited about anything.

His mom and Dr. Lingstrom didn't act excited, either. They were quiet and sedate, even when they sang the usual "Happy Creation Day" song. Neither Billy's mom nor Dr. Lingstrom seemed to enjoy the meal. Billy didn't enjoy it, either. It was just what his system required; therefore, he ingested it.

It had taken five years of experimentation for Billy to discover the appropriate foods for his animatronic system. During those years, he ate whatever his mom put on his plate. Like or dislike didn't come into the issue, although his taste sensors indicated some foods were "better" than others.

After the five years testing foods, Billy had concluded that color had no place in animatronic food. The colors in food tended to overload his circuits. Therefore, he required all of his food to be white.

"White?" Billy's mom had said the afternoon he'd informed her of his conclusion. She'd been fixing him his usual snack of a peanut butter and jelly sandwich.

"I will consume this sandwich," Billy told her, "because social convention dictates that I eat what you have already prepared. However, from this point forward, I require all white foods."

"White," his mom repeated.

"Animatronics do not efficiently digest color," Billy told his mom.

His mom had stood, walked to the refrigerator, and

opened it. She spent several seconds staring at its contents. Then she did the same with the cabinets. When she turned around, tears ran down her cheeks.

Billy was aware that tears indicated sadness. He, therefore, processed the potential reasons for his mom's unhappiness. It took just a few seconds to conclude that she was unhappy because she didn't have the right foods. She would have to go out and buy them.

Billy's mom did go out and buy the foods, and for the last eight years, Billy had eaten nothing but white foods: white flour-based breads and other baked goods, white rice, potatoes, white pasta, white sauces (usually cheese-based), grits, cooked (but not browned) chicken or fish or turkey, white mushrooms and onions, cauliflower, and apples (peeled, of course).

Billy's mom was concerned that these foods didn't give Billy enough "fiber." He researched the subject and discovered that fiber was something that was needed by the human digestive system. Because Billy's animatronic system was designed to be similar to a human's, Billy reasoned he might require fiber, too. He, therefore, asked his mom to purchase a powdered fiber supplement (white, of course), which she dissolved in his water or his milk.

The same year Billy reached conclusions about his diet, he settled on his appropriate wardrobe as well. Billy's clothing had been something of an issue for some time. He had never thought the clothing his mom asked him to wear fit his animatronic presence. Yes, he knew that animatronics could and often did wear costumes, but

Billy wanted to be a more autonomous animatronic. He required his own unique look.

Since Billy knew himself to be made of metal, even if his external appearance didn't appear metallic, he reached the conclusion that various shades of silver and dark gray were required for his clothing. The lines of the clothing had to be simple, resembling the sleek flat surfaces of metal.

So, on Billy's thirteenth (eighteenth) creation day, he and his mom and Dr. Lingstrom ate white pasta with white sauce and cauliflower with homemade ranch dressing (it had to be homemade because the store-bought variety had too many flecks of green). Billy was satisfied with the meal. The fact that his mom and Dr. Lingstrom left over half their small portions on their plates informed Billy that they found the meal less satisfying than he did.

After the obligatory blowing out of the candles on the cake and opening of the presents (which included some additions to his silver-and-gray wardrobe and a new laptop computer that his mom said would interface well with his internal processors), Billy thanked his mom and Dr. Lingstrom for the creation day celebration, and he left the kitchen to return to his private space in the basement.

As Billy reached the door that opened onto the long, steep flight of stairs leading to his space, he heard Dr. Lingstrom speak.

"Don't you think enough is enough, Vera?" Dr. Lingstrom asked. "He's eighteen. It's time for him to go into the group home. The one I told you about has a couple residents with severe delusions. One has lycan-thropy and one—"

"I'm not putting him in a home," Billy's mom said. "This is his home."

"But you've given up so much," Dr. Lingstrom said. "You've lost your husband and your social life. You told me yourself that I'm your only remaining friend. And forgive me for being rude, but you don't look so good. You're losing your health, too."

"You think I don't know all that?" Billy's mom said. "I know. But . . . he's my son."

Billy always felt a boost of energy through his systems when he heard his mom say, "He's my son." It confirmed that he was still properly fulfilling his function as an ani-matronic designed to be a son.

Once Billy's mom concluded her conversation with Dr. Lingstrom, Billy opened the door to the basement. He walked down the stairs to his space.

Billy's move from his small bedroom to the larger and more secluded basement had occurred on his seventh (twelfth) creation day. That was the year he'd informed his mom that an animatronic required isolation and dark-ness for optimal recharging. Minimal auditory input was needed as well. Billy's bedroom, which was at the front of the house, was too near the street for quiet. Billy's auditory sensors were always registering the passage of cars, the barking of dogs, and the screaming of playing children.

The basement, insulated by its thick cinder-block

walls and the earth that surrounded them, muffled much of the exterior sounds. In the basement, Billy's networks were given the silence necessary to shut down and reboot each day.

When Billy set up his own personal recharging and service area in the basement, he'd done so with placid tranquility in mind. Removing the old shag brown carpeting and disposing of stored boxes and secondhand furniture, Billy had scrubbed the basement's cement floor and its cinder-block walls. Both of these surfaces were naturally gray, so Billy didn't paint them. He moved his metal recharging platform to the basement, and he'd requested that his mom buy him a metal table and chair for his information download station. This was where his computer and the books he was currently reading were kept.

After his thirteenth (eighteenth) creation day celebration, Billy went directly to his download station. He wanted to update his knowledge base to include the definition of *lycanthropy*.

Not long after Billy's thirteenth (eighteenth) creation day, on a morning that Billy's sensors informed him was windy and rainy, Billy opened the door at the top of the basement stairs. He walked purposefully, as usual, to the kitchen to await the morning's hot cereal.

When Billy left his charging station in the mornings to go to the kitchen for his morning nourishment, he always heard his mom moving around in the room. He would hear her clinking dishes or running water or closing cabinet doors.

This morning, however, he didn't hear any of those things.

Billy's auditory sensors reported to him the sound of the rain thrumming on the roof and the sound of heavy sheets of rainwater being slapped against the living room windows. From out in the street, he heard the *sshhh* of car tires sluicing through the rain on the pavement. But these sounds were all his sensors were receiving.

Billy, his systems flipping through subfolders to find a potential reason for his mom's silence, came up with no explanation for what he was hearing (or not hearing). He, therefore, walked into the kitchen to gather more data.

Nothing in the kitchen, however, was useful. The kitchen looked as it always did, yellow and white, neat and tidy. From his reading, Billy had concluded that his mom was a "good housekeeper." She kept everything clean and orderly.

Still seeking data to explain the unusual morning, Billy opened the door leading into the garage. The family car was in the garage. His mom was not.

Billy went down the hall to his mom's room. As it always did during the day, the door to her bedroom stood open. When Billy looked in, he found the room empty, the bed made.

Billy went down the hall to look in his mom's office. It, too, was as organized as always—all books and files stored neatly on white shelves or in white filing cabinets—and it, too, lacked his mom.

Billy looked into his old bedroom. It was empty. He'd already looked into the living room and dining room. This left the bathroom.

Billy walked down the hall and hesitated in front of the bathroom door.

One of Billy's largest subprograms was the one assigned to human manners and behavior. In order to be a "son," Billy had to properly perform a son's functions. This meant doing what human boys (and as the years went by, teens) did properly. One of the things in this subroutine was the fact that it was wrong to walk in on your mom when she was in the bathroom.

The bathroom door was closed. Because she wasn't in any other room in the house, probability suggested his mom was in the bathroom.

Billy knocked on the bathroom door. "Mom?" Billy called through the closed door. "It is Billy. Are you coming to the kitchen to prepare my breakfast?"

Billy's mom did not answer.

Billy's auditory processors were having trouble determining for certain because of the noise interference from the rain and wind, but no sounds seemed to be coming from the bathroom. If his mom was in the room, she was silent.

Billy did a quick run through the systems assigned to unusual occurrences. These systems included subfolders filled with information on emergencies. Billy had gotten the information from several books.

After shifting through his data banks, Billy concluded he had to enter the bathroom. His mom might need his help.

Billy lifted a sturdy hand and knocked on the door again. When he received no response, he opened it.

As soon as Billy opened the bathroom door, his sensors were overwhelmed with a variety of input. Although part of the information was normal—his olfactory sensors reported that the room had a lavender scent, which it always did after his mom was in the room—most of what his sensors recorded were things he'd never encountered before. All this new information came through his visual sensors.

Billy's visual sensors informed Billy that the gleaming white bathtub was filled with water, almost to the brim. Billy's mom was in the water. Or more accurately, she was *under* the water.

Billy could see his mom's face just beneath the surface of the still, clear liquid. His mom's blonde hair wafted around her head, partially obscuring her staring eyes. Her body, unclothed—something Billy had never seen before—was limp.

Billy's extensive reading had installed in his database what he needed to conclude that his mom was dead. But why? Billy had learned that humans always wanted to know why a person had died.

Billy turned away from his mom's corpse and looked at the rest of the room. Outside, thunder rumbled as Billy's sensors registered an empty drinking glass on the gray granite counter by the sink. He noted the open medicine cabinet.

Billy reached a conclusion and filed the information in the appropriate file. He then did what his databases told him was the right thing to do in this situation; he left the bathroom and went to the phone to dial 911.

One of the things Billy's mom had downloaded into Billy's databases not long before she died was the imperative that Billy no longer inform people that he was an animatronic. Billy's robotic identity, she told him, must from that point on be a secret.

"I'm going to update your programming," his mom had told him. She'd picked up his silver hairbrush and begun brushing Billy's thick brown hair.

This was how Billy's mom always changed his programming. She'd explained this to him the first year of his existence as an animatronic. When she brushed his hair, she'd told him, his hardware received its updates.

The update regarding Billy's secret robot identity had two parts. First, Billy was to keep his animatronic nature to himself. Second, he was to do his best to mimic normal human behavior when he had to be around people.

"But I am an animatronic," Billy had said while his mom installed his new programming.

"I understand that," his mom had said. "However, from now on, others don't need to know that."

Because of this programming, Billy didn't inform the police and other officials who came in response to his 911 call that he was an animatronic. Some of them, however, already knew. The town Billy lived in was small, and he was the only animatronic living in it. Anyone who had lived in the town for long knew of Billy.

The day Billy's mom died, though, no one spoke to him about what he was. Everyone who came to the house just went about their business and left, speaking to Billy very little. Only one young female EMT asked Billy if he was going to be all right.

"He'll be fine, Fran," another, older EMT said, tugging on Fran's arm. "Come on. Let's get out of here."

Billy's face recognition programming informed him that the older EMT was the father of a boy Billy used to call a friend. Billy considered telling the man to say hi to his son (this kind of communication was in Billy's social skills subroutines), but he concluded that emergency situation protocols trumped social protocols.

Billy said nothing as the EMTs left the house with his mom's body. He just closed and locked the door and went into the bathroom to clean it. That was what his mom would have wanted him to do.

He then went down to the basement. He needed to interface with his computer so he could read the file that his mom had told him to read if she died.

Billy sat in his gleaming silver metal chair, and he accessed his computer's files. As he waited for the one that he wanted to open, his memory banks brought up the image of his mom telling him about the file.

They'd been sitting at the table eating. Billy had been eating rice and chicken and cauliflower. His mom had been eating tiny bites of a package meal that she'd taken from the freezer and microwaved.

At one point, Billy's mom had set down her fork.

She'd turned and looked directly at Billy. "Billy, there's something you need to add to your database," she'd said.

Billy had stopped eating. He'd focused on his mom's words so he could integrate whatever she said into his system.

"Before dinner, I emailed you a file," Billy's mom said. Her face scrunched up unusually for a moment. Then it returned to its most recent normal. She cleared her throat. "You are not to open the file unless I am dead." She squinted at Billy. "Does that compute?"

Billy nodded. "Do not open the file unless you are dead."

Billy's mom wiped her eyes. "Right. Just download the file to your computer and keep it. If I die, read the file. It will have the next set of updates you'll need."

Billy had nodded and given his mom his programmed polite response. "Thank you, Mom."

Now Billy opened the file.

The file was a big one. It took some time for Billy to read it. It was full of information Billy had not had before. It was useful information.

Now that his mom was dead, the file informed Billy he had to be a different animatronic. He could no longer be an animatronic son. He had to be an animatronic adult. This required a completely different set of subroutines than the son animatronic had. His mom's file installed those subroutines. It gave him instructions on how to purchase what he needed to eat and care for the home, how to cook food, how to shop online, how to pay bills, how to hire people to take care of the house, the yard, and the car. It informed him that he had a substantial financial account (an inheritance) that would fund his needs for the rest of his life. This had come from investments (something that Billy understood because he'd continued to read books on the subject after those first books that were "too old" for him).

Billy immediately began acting on his new programming. He became an animatronic adult.

Over the next year, which Billy noted only because the other houses in his neighborhood put out the lights on their trees—signifying the arrival of Christmas, Billy's adult animatronic existence was focused primarily on mastering his new programming. He had learned much, but he found that he needed to practice what he'd learned many times to become proficient at executing it.

Once Billy was comfortable with his new knowledge and skills, though, he discovered that he was experiencing what felt like incoherence in his system. Billy's reading suggested that this incoherence might have been a condition called "cognitive dissonance."

Cognitive dissonance, Billy had learned, was the mental unrest that occurred when a being (usually a human) held conflicting beliefs or attitudes. The reason Billy concluded that he had this condition was that his senses were reporting to him two states of reality that were at odds with each other.

Billy, being an animatronic, didn't exactly have beliefs or attitudes, but he did have a sense of self. And he was beginning to recognize that his sense of self was fractured. On the one hand, Billy knew himself to be a robot. On the other hand, his sensory experience of himself was that of a human being. In other words, Billy was a robot, but his physical systems were like those of a human. This was becoming more and more unsettling to Billy. He decided he had to do something about it.

Billy's decision to create coherence was a catalyst for a lot of research over the coming days. How could he create consistency between what he knew himself to be and what his senses reported him to be?

After reading and exploring potential options, Billy concluded that he needed to replace his human-appearing arms and legs with limbs that were more animatronic-like. From what Billy concluded based on his research, this meant he needed to switch out his current arms and legs for prosthetic arms and legs. This, Billy learned after even more research, required surgery.

Thanks to his mom, Billy was familiar with seeking services from other humans. He knew how to use the computer to look for what he needed. He did this now, finding a list of surgeons in his area. Starting with the top name on the list, he dialed the assigned number.

When a friendly woman's voice answered the phone, Billy stated his needs. "Hello, my name is Billy. I am seeking a surgeon who will remove my arms and legs and replace them with prosthetics."

Billy's auditory sensors registered the sound of a gasp coming through the phone. The woman, not sounding as friendly, asked, "Why do you need all your limbs removed? Do you have a systemic infection?"

Billy ran this question through his processor. "No, I

have no infection. I have cognitive dissonance, and my limbs are not consistent with my identity." Billy was careful not to say that his identity was animatronic because he was still running his mom's programming regarding keeping his robotic nature a secret.

A dial tone suddenly buzzed in Billy's ear. This informed him that the woman had hung up.

Billy moved on to the next number.

Forty minutes later, Billy had gone through every surgeon in the region surrounding his small town. He had received responses similar to the first one from every office he called.

What was the next logical step?

Billy got up and laid down on his recharging station. He felt like his systems were depleted. Perhaps when he rebooted, he would be able to find the surgeon he needed.

The process that led Billy to a surgeon ended up being far more protracted than the steps of his original plan. This was because his current programming was deficient in the intricacies of how surgery, and the medical system in general, functioned. Billy had to access an extensive network of new databases before he located a surgeon who agreed to perform the required operations, in a city within driving distance.

Billy concluded, after an exhaustive search, that licensed surgeons would not perform the surgeries Billy required. Logically, Billy decided, this meant that an unlicensed surgeon might be able to provide the needed service. Accordingly, Billy began searching for such a surgeon and he found one—a "disreputable" doctor who had lost his license because of malpractice lawsuits related to unspecified substance abuse and health issues—who was willing to do any surgeries asked of him . . . if the fee satisfied him. When Billy's data downloads led him to the man—"just call me Doc," the fee requested was well within the budget Billy had assigned to his project.

"This isn't going to happen overnight, you know," Doc told Billy over the phone after he agreed to proceed with Billy's plan. Doc coughed heavily. "Every time we lop off a limb, your body will need time to recover. You won't be able to be fitted with a prosthetic until the stump is healed." Doc coughed again. The sound was loud and crackly to Billy's auditory processors. "You'll need someone to help you while you heal," Doc went on. "And when you get your prosthetic, you'll need physical therapy to adapt to it."

"I will not require healing time or therapy," Billy told the doctor.

"What? Are you superhuman or something?" Doc asked.

Billy wanted to explain that he was an animatronic, but that would have gone against his programming. Therefore, he just said, "I am Billy, and I will adapt easily."

Doc laughed, which triggered a cascade of coughing. Finally, he said, "Yeah, well, humor an old man. I'm going to set up the back room and call in my squeeze, Norma, to take care of you if you need it. Norma's retired. Used to be a nurse. Sometimes she helps me out. She can do it all—recovery and physical therapy." Doc laughed in a way Billy had never heard before. The sound was similar to that of the machine gun fire Billy's auditory sensors had picked up from the TV. "Multitalented, my Norma," Doc said.

Doc gave Billy an address, and Billy told Doc he would arrive the next day. Doc coughed again and said, "I'll be waiting."

Billy was an animatronic, so he was never thankful. But he was able to experience a sort of satisfaction when the information he needed was there when he needed it. He received this satisfaction the next day when he went out to the garage and got in the family station wagon.

Because of Billy's mom, Billy was able to drive the old station wagon that sat in his garage. His mom had added this skill to his database two years before his thirteenth (eighteenth) creation day.

Billy had not used the skill often since he'd acquired it, but he was able to easily call up the appropriate functions when he got in the station wagon to head to the city to see Doc. By the time Billy passed the junkyard that sat at the edge of his town, Billy was confident that he was in satisfactory control of the vehicle. And he was right. The drive to the city went smoothly, and Billy found Doc's location easily.

Like Billy, Doc lived in a basement. Unlike Billy's, though, Doc's was under seven floors of an empty old brick building that used to be a mental hospital. Doc had laughed and laughed when he'd told Billy this. Billy was unable to figure out, from his available knowledge, why this was so funny.

When skinny and gray-haired Doc met Billy outside the dirty building with the boarded-up windows and the crumbling concrete steps, Doc told Billy he owned the building. Doc waved at the building with a hand that shook slightly. He coughed as he said, "Got it cheap because no one else wants it. Don't keep it up, so it's easy to maintain."

Doc had Billy park his car behind the building. Then Doc led Billy into the building through a gray metal door. Billy thought the door was appropriate for the entrance to a place where an animatronic would receive service.

Once inside the building, Doc led Billy down a long flight of dust-covered and trash-littered stairs. Billy's visual sensors registered a small rodent—probability predicted a rat—scuttling along the landing as they passed it.

Although Billy's research regarding surgery had inputted into his system images of clean and modern surgical suites and equipment, Doc's premises didn't concern Billy. Billy was an animatronic. He didn't require perfect conditions for servicing.

Doc led Billy to a small room with no windows. The room had peeling beige paint and one narrow metal-framed bed with a thin mattress. It wasn't a traditional charging platform, but it would suffice.

"Are you sure you want to do this?" Doc asked Billy as Billy inspected the room.

Billy rotated to gaze at Doc. "I have chosen a course of action that is the right one for me."

Doc chuckled. "Okey-dokey. Whatever floats your boat. Got the money?"

Billy handed over the cash Doc had requested.

"We'll get it done first thing in the morning," Doc said.

Billy was an animatronic. He didn't get excited. But he registered something that might have been anticipation that night before he lay down on the yellowing bare mattress to recharge his systems.

Billy's anticipation did not correlate with the events that unfolded after his first surgery. The information he'd inputted into his database, he concluded, had been lacking.

As an animatronic, Billy did not experience pain. He did, however, have tactile senses that reported pain-like awareness from time to time. Not long after his second (seventh) creation day, for example, Billy had fallen in front of his house. He had skinned his knee. It was interesting to experience the stinging sensation and watch the blood flow from his skin as tears had leaked from his eyes. Billy had not chosen any of these reactions; he had to assume they were programmed. The blood and tears were not welcome. They were inconsistent with being the kind of animatronic that Billy wanted to be.

Billy was not expecting what his programming had in store after Doc removed Billy's left leg. The pain-like awareness and the flows of blood that he experienced were far greater than that of the skinned knee. Billy discovered that he was programmed to cry and yell out when his thigh reported to him sensations that he defined (based on his reading) as agony. He also discovered that his programming allowed the raw and bloody tissues that made up his "stump" to become inflamed with infection. This resulted in a cascade failure of many of Billy's systems. His temperature rose quite high. His digestive system shut down. His neuro-processing capabilities were compromised.

Fortunately, all this wasn't permanent.

White-haired, heavily tanned, and large-handed Norma, who took care of Billy after the surgery, told Billy that he "bounced back" pretty quickly "all things considered." Billy was not able to determine what that meant. But Norma did tell him after four weeks that he was ready to be fitted with his first prosthetic.

Doc had ordered all Billy's prosthetics using the money that Billy gave him. Billy had shown him a picture of dark-gray-metal-and-plastic prosthetics. Those were the ones that Billy required.

Billy's visual sensors reported to Billy that the look of his new leg prosthetic was acceptable. The feel of it—as reported by his tactile sensors—was not.

After doing his research, Billy had projected that his new prosthetic limb would make him stronger and faster. It would make him a better animatronic. Billy's research, however, must have been inaccurate or incomplete. The prosthetic not only did not increase his strength or speed, it did the opposite.

Billy found that his ability to get around was greatly

compromised by the new metal-and-plastic leg. Although it was strong on its own, the metal and plastic limb lacked efficiency when combined with the stump left at the top of Billy's old (and no-longer-there) leg. Billy's gait, which had been previously smooth and upright, became hesitant and faltering.

Billy told Doc the result had not been what he'd expected.

"No refunds," Doc said. "But we can stop with one leg. You want to call it quits?"

"No, I do not," Billy said. "I have concluded that this unsatisfactory movement is the result of the partially finished servicing. After the other limbs have been replaced, I will function correctly."

Doc laughed, coughed, and said, "Whatever you say, kid."

Although Billy wanted to go ahead immediately with the next limb replacement, Doc refused. "I don't care what you say, kid," Doc said. "Your body needs time to heal and adjust to the shock before we move on."

Billy opened his mouth to object, but Doc held up a hand. "Yeah, I know you're different. But what I say goes. If you kick the bucket because we push it, I won't get my whole fee." Doc cackled. (Billy had discovered that the right word for his funny laugh was *cackle*.)

"Go home," Doc said. "Get used to this new leg. Come back in a few months if you still want to go ahead with it. We'll do the next one." He coughed and wiped his thin mouth with the back of his shaky hand.

Because Billy knew that Doc was the only surgeon who would do what Billy wanted, he was forced to go along with Doc's plan. After spending six weeks with Doc and Norma, Billy got in his car and drove home.

The drive home was harder than the drive to Doc's. The new limb made working the pedals awkward.

Billy was relieved when he passed the junkyard. It meant he was just a couple miles from his house. As he drove by the mountains of discarded rubbish and the rusted and crushed vehicles, Billy's processors conjured an image of Billy's rejected parts tossed in among the debris. The thought satisfied him for some reason. It made him feel like he was on his way to becoming the whole and complete animatronic he wanted to be.

After Billy's first leg replacement, Billy learned that his basement recharging area was no longer going to suit him. The long flight of stairs was too difficult to negotiate with the new prosthetic leg. Accordingly, Billy hired a moving service to remove his parents' bedroom furniture, and bring up Billy's metal platform, table, and chair from the basement. These were placed in the now-empty bedroom.

Because this bedroom, unlike Billy's old room, was at the back of the house, Billy's auditory sensors could handle the noise level. Plus, even if the noise level wasn't ideal, Billy's olfactory sensors provided feedback that made the room more than satisfactory; they reported the scent of lavender—something that triggered in Billy's memory banks images of his mom. The images compensated for any increase in the noise level over that of the basement. Besides, the most important reason for using this room as his recharging area was that it removed the need for negotiating stairs.

Billy's second limb replacement was his left arm. That went better than the first one. Billy found that the substitute arm, though not as efficient as his original one, functioned well enough to allow Billy to perform his daily tasks.

The third limb replacement—the second leg, however, was even less satisfactory than the first and second surgeries. With both original legs gone, Billy discovered that he was weaker and less coordinated than ever.

Billy also began experiencing pain-like sensations constantly. At the junction between his remaining flesh and bone and the prosthetic connections, Billy's tactile sensors reported a chronic burning ache. They also reported erroneously similar sensations in the missing limbs. Billy knew that his new limbs had no tactile sensors, so he should "feel" nothing from them. But he did. The resulting abundance of pain-like sensory input was more than a little distracting.

Why was this project failing to meet Billy's expected goals? Was Doc the problem?

Billy used all his computing capacity to tackle these questions. In the end, he determined that Doc, although old and shaky and not as clean as a normal surgeon would be, was not the problem. The problem had to be, Billy concluded, his own shortcomings.

Billy hoped the last limb replacement would remove all the problems he was having with his updated endoskeleton. But it did not. It simply added to his overall lack of coordination and weakness, and it exacerbated the overabundance of input from his tactile sensors.

Two days after Billy's fifteenth (twentieth) creation day, Doc drove Billy home following Billy's last limb replacement. Doc drove because Billy's new arms and legs did not make safe driving possible. Norma followed the station wagon in a battered old white pickup so she could take Doc back to the city after he left Billy at his house.

Once inside his home again, Billy jerked his way through the living room and lurched into the kitchen. His progress was slow and destructive. He gouged the walls, knocked over two lamps, and scraped the hard-wood floors along the way.

When Billy reached the kitchen, he fumbled for a glass and dropped it. The glass shattered. Shards went everywhere.

Billy managed to open a different cabinet. He got out a plastic cup. Slopping water all over the place, Billy filled the cup halfway. He lunged over to the table and dropped into a chair. There, he applied all his processing capacity to his problem.

Billy had to accept the failure of his endeavor. The reality was that although Billy was replacing his limbs, there was still a vast disconnect between his animatronic nature and his body's more humanlike systems. He had to find a way to remedy these inconsistencies.

The day after Doc returned Billy—with all new limbs—to Billy's house, Billy spent hours online researching his options for further modifications. In the course of this research, he happened upon an online chat room for people who weren't satisfied with their physical appearance. In the chatroom, he met Maliah.

Billy had never encountered the name Maliah, so he asked Maliah what her name meant.

"It's a Hawaiian name," Maliah responded. "My mom told me it means 'of the sea.' My dad said it means 'bitter.' Figures he'd say that. He wasn't a nice man."

Since his seventh (twelfth) creation day, Billy had engaged in only minimal interaction with anyone other than his mom or Dr. Lingstrom (and after his mom had died, Billy didn't see Dr. Lingstrom, either). This lack of contact with people wasn't a problem. However, Billy discovered that his neural networks expanded greatly as a result of his interactions with Maliah. He was so satisfied, in fact, by his communications with Maliah that he stopped researching further physical enhancements. He wanted to integrate what he was learning about interpersonal communication.

"My dad hit me all the time," Maliah typed on the second night that she and Billy chatted online. "So of course, I went and got in a relationship with a jerk who picked up where my dad left off."

Billy found Maliah's words challenging. She used a lot of vernacular and clichés that Billy had to look up. His contact with her vastly expanded his vocabulary of casual slang.

"After that," Maliah wrote, "I just ping-ponged from one abusive jerk to the next."

"I am sorry," Billy typed back. He was reasonably certain this was the right response.

Maliah responded with a smile emoticon. Billy deduced that he'd gotten it right.

After that, Maliah typed, "Are you an abusive jerk?" She put a winking emoticon after the question.

Billy wasn't sure how to interpret that. He decided to answer the question honestly.

"I am not an abusive jerk."

Maliah sent him a laughing emoticon.

Was that good?

This type of interaction was quite stimulating to Billy's processors. It required that he use his databases in ways he'd never used them before.

"Why are you in this chatroom?" Maliah typed next. "What do you want to change about your body?"

Billy had to think about this question. He was still running his "secret robot" programming. He couldn't tell her the truth, not all of it anyway. Billy typed, "I want my body to match who I really am on the inside."

"Oh, that's cool," Maliah typed. "Me too. On the inside, I'm a beach babe. On the outside, I'm pudgy and have a flat face. I want liposuction and cheek sculpting and a nose job."

Billy did not know how to respond to this. His social subroutines informed him that commenting on a girl's appearance was quite complex. He could easily cause "hurt feelings" if he responded incorrectly.

Maliah saved his circuits when she didn't wait for a response. "What work do you want done?"

Maliah's desire for cheek sculpting had triggered a

conclusion in Billy's processors. "I want facial sculpting, too," Billy typed.

Metal plates, Billy realized. This was what he needed next.

Now that he looked very much like his dad had when his dad left, Billy understood that the curves of his face were not remotely consistent with an animatronic appearance. If he could have metal plates implanted under his skin, however, his face would take on the angular planes he thought were more in keeping with his animatronic nature.

Billy wanted to stop chatting with Maliah so he could call Doc to talk about this new idea. Maliah, however, was typing again.

"Do you want to meet in person?" she asked.

Billy thought about this. It could be interesting, he concluded.

"Yes, I do."

As Maliah pulled up to the small house set in a row of similar houses, she asked herself, for at least the twentieth time, if she'd lost her mind. She was about to meet a guy she'd met online, and she'd agreed to meet him at his house. Was she insane? He could be a serial killer, and she was about to serve herself up to him like a juicy roast.

Maliah let her car idle as she craned her neck to look through the passenger window. She studied the house.

It looked okay, she figured. The yard was neat; the lawn was green and mowed, and the bushes were trimmed. The house had clean white siding. The windows were sparkling. It didn't look like the lair of a serial killer. But then, what did a serial killer's lair look like?

"Oh, just get on with it," Maliah told herself. "If he kills you, it will save you money in surgeries. You won't have to try to look good enough for someone better than a serial killer."

Maliah snorted at her dumb joke. She got out of the car and treaded briskly up the walk before she could talk herself out of what she was doing.

Standing on a white-painted porch, Maliah took a deep breath. She rang the doorbell.

The door opened almost immediately. Billy must have been watching for her.

As soon as the door opened, Maliah put on her best smile and hoped Billy would see her even white teeth instead of her wide nose and her double chin. She'd taken care with her eye makeup, and she knew her eyes were her best feature, so she felt pretty good about her big brown eyes. Her chestnut-colored Hawaiian skin was a positive, too. She had a great complexion. Hopefully, he'd focus on that as well.

The first thing Maliah registered when she looked up at the man standing in front of her was that he was tall. He towered over her. The second thing she noticed was that he had a really cute face. That was a surprise. Yeah, his cheeks were a bit chipmunk-y—maybe that was why he wanted some facial sculpting done—but all in all, he was pretty good-looking.

Maliah dropped her gaze to check out Billy's body. Her smile faltered.

The man standing before her wore a short-sleeve gray shirt, and extending from the open sleeves were two gray prosthetic arms that ended in prosthetic hands with articulated fingers. Arms, plural. Both of his arms were artificial. Wow. Why hadn't Billy mentioned he was missing his arms? It was so . . . heart-rending.

Maliah's eyes moistened. She blinked, hoping Billy hadn't seen her pity. She smiled at him. He needed someone to accept him as he was, not feel sorry for him. She could give him that acceptance. This was a man who needed her. She liked that idea.

But should she say anything about his prosthetics? Should she ask what happened?

"Hello," Billy said. "I am happy that you are here."

Billy's voice didn't match his words. His voice was flat and lacked inflection—it was like the voice of a robot.

Although Maliah hadn't said anything yet, Billy spoke again. "You look very nice," he said. "That is a pretty purple dress."

Maliah looked back up to Billy's face. He was smiling at her as if he was pleased with what he saw. That made her feel good, and she was happy she could see his smile because the flat tone of his voice belied his words and expression. He sounded a little robotic, but no one could help how they sounded.

Maliah found her own voice. "Um, hi," she said. She didn't mention his arms.

"Please come in," Billy said. "I ordered a white cake. White is the only color I eat. I used to bake my own cakes, but my new limbs do not work satisfactorily."

Billy raised his arms and then gestured at his legs. He stepped back from the door in an awkward backward lunge-like move. Maliah looked down at Billy's legs.

Billy's legs were hidden inside a pair of gray slacks, but the slacks were tight enough to reveal the unnatural outlines of his limbs. Were Billy's legs prosthetic, too?

Maliah couldn't contain herself. She blurted the question.

Billy nodded placidly. "I had all my limbs replaced. The result was not as I expected it would be, but I am adapting."

Maliah teared up again. She wiped her eyes, stepped forward, and put her hand on Billy's shoulder. "I really admire your attitude. You're very brave."

What an amazing man, Maliah thought. Most men would be resentful or angry if they'd gone through whatever it was Billy had gone through, but Billy obviously didn't feel sorry for himself at all. Instead of acting like a victim, he was being a perfect gentleman. How cool was that? Every other guy Maliah had been with had acted like a smartass from the get-go. No wonder they'd been losers. They'd never treated her with respect. Billy was treating her with respect.

Limbless and flat-voiced or not, Billy was better than the guys that Maliah had dated up until now. Maliah's smile widened. "It's nice to meet you, Billy. I'm happy to be here."

Maliah entered Billy's house, and she was glad to see that it looked as nice on the inside as it did on the outside. A guy who could keep a clean house. Go figure. She was also delighted—and surprised—that she enjoyed the two hours she spent having white cake and milk in Billy's spotless kitchen.

When Maliah left Billy, she promised she'd come back again, and she intended to keep the promise. In the past, she probably would have given Billy a pass. His android-like voice was a little disconcerting, and his lack of limbs made him pitch and reel all over the place when he walked—like he was walking on the deck of a ship in a tropical storm. But Maliah had learned the hard way that the superficial stuff didn't matter as much as the stuff you couldn't see. In spite of his obvious limitations, Billy had had two qualities Maliah really liked. Three actually. One, he listened when she talked. He really listened. His gaze never left her face when she spoke, as if what she was saying was the most important thing in the world. Two, when he talked, he was interesting. He was obviously well-read. That was a nice change of pace from the idiots Maliah usually went out with. And three, he was nice to her. He was very kind.

Maliah figured she could do worse. In fact, she already had done worse. Much, much worse.

The addition of Maliah in Billy's life took up a lot of his time. This, he concluded, was a good thing. It expanded his knowledge base even more. It gave him a new purpose as well.

After Maliah's third visit to his house, Maliah asked him what he was to her. This was a baffling question at first. Maliah was many things. She was a human. She was a woman. She was a visitor in Billy's house. What did she mean? What was the right response?

This was why Billy liked his time with Maliah. She forced him to think in ways his processors had never thought in before.

Before Billy had to attempt a reply, Maliah clarified her question. "I mean, are we just friends, or am I your girlfriend?" Her face flushed a little.

Billy knew that flushed faces could mean embarrassment. He didn't want Maliah to be embarrassed. His reading had indicated that humans didn't like being embarrassed.

"You are my girlfriend," Billy said. This was true. She was a girl, and she was his friend.

Maliah gave Billy a huge smile. Then she leaned in and kissed him right on the mouth.

Billy's neuro processing system concluded two things from the kiss. One, kissing was an experience worth having more than once. Second, Maliah was indeed Billy's girlfriend. He found this satisfying.

As satisfying as having a girlfriend was, however, Billy still was unsettled by his failure to live up to his robotic potential. He needed to continue with his self-improvement plan. To that end, he called Doc.

"Hey, kid," Doc said after coughing into Billy's auditory sensors. "How're the new limbs?"

"My improved limbs have not improved me as much I expected them to," Billy said. "I require additional work."

Doc coughed again. "What do you want now? Much as I have no trouble taking your money, you don't have any more appendages to swap out."

"An angular facial structure would be more consistent with my internal nature," Billy said. "I require metal plates implanted over my cheekbones, under the skin, to achieve that structure."

Doc coughed, then breathed heavily into the phone for several seconds. "Yeah, okay, I can do that."

Doc named a fee. Billy agreed to it. They also agreed on a date.

Billy called Maliah. "I am leaving to have surgery in two days. I will contact you when I get back."

"Oh, okay," Maliah said. "Do you want me to come with you?"

"No, thank you," Billy said.

Actually, Billy would have been okay with Maliah's company, but Doc had inputted into Billy's system instructions similar to those of Billy's mom: Billy was not to tell anyone about Doc or the surgeries he did in the basement of the old mental hospital. Doc's work and his address were both secrets.

"Okay. Call me when you get back," Maliah said. "I'll come take care of you."

"That sounds nice. Thank you," Billy said.

It was a week before Billy could call Maliah. After the surgery, Billy's face swelled up to twice its normal size. The incisions Doc made in Billy's cheeks wouldn't stop bleeding, and they leaked a greenish pus that Norma said they had to stop before Billy could go home. Norma made Billy swallow a lot of antibiotics, and she changed the gauze dressings on his face multiple times before finally agreeing that Doc could take Billy back to his house.

Billy, checking the results of the latest procedure in the mirror, thought the metal plates were 50 percent effective and 50 percent ineffective. They did make his face squarer and more animatronic-like. However, they also left him with jagged and livid red scars that were more reminiscent of a monster than they were of a robot. These scars also added to the already-copious amount of his pain-like sensations. He had to research more options. He hadn't yet achieved his goal.

Maliah apparently agreed with Billy's assessment. When she arrived that evening to take care of Billy, the smile she wore when he opened the door disappeared the instant that she looked at him. "Oh," she said.

"I am not done yet," Billy said. "The next set of modifications will get me closer to my goal."

Maliah didn't come in the house when Billy opened the door wider. She covered her mouth and blinked rapidly.

"Are you coming in?" Billy asked.

Maliah took a deep breath. "I think you need your incisions cleaned."

Maliah came into the house, but she barely glanced at Billy as she passed him and went into the kitchen. Billy closed the front door and started following Maliah.

Even though Billy had been practicing walking with his prosthetics, he still didn't move as fast as Maliah did.

She was in the kitchen running water when he got to the doorway. And she was talking to herself.

"What was he thinking?" she muttered. "His face isn't cute anymore."

Billy found this statement helpful. It suggested that he was closer to his goal than he thought he was. He didn't want to be cute. He wanted to be robotic.

Although Maliah didn't come over as often after Billy modified his face, she still talked to him frequently. They were on the phone nearly every day. Even so, Billy didn't tell Maliah when he made arrangements with Doc to have the whites of his eyes dyed black.

"It's a very dangerous and painful procedure, kid," Doc said the day after Billy proposed the idea. "I looked into it, and I can do it. But I can't use the usual anesthetic because of potential toxic interactions. Are you sure?"

"I am sure," Billy said.

A week later, Doc picked Billy up and took him back to the basement of the abandoned mental hospital. There, Doc used needles to insert black dye into the irises and whites of Billy's eyes. The injections triggered Billy's sensory processors, which activated his vocal systems; Billy screamed during the entire procedure.

When Billy returned home, he was gratified by what he saw in the mirror. This procedure was the most successful so far. His eyes, as he had intended them to be, were now pitch-black.

Billy called Maliah and asked her to come and see his

eyes. She didn't sound enthusiastic about the idea, but she agreed.

When Maliah arrived and looked at Billy, she seemed happier with his eyes than she had been with his facial plates. Looking up at his eyes (Maliah was very short), Maliah said, "Well, I miss your big brown eyes, but I have to admit that looks kind of cool. Sort of vampirish."

Billy wasn't sure that vampirish was good. He was a robot, not a vampire.

He had to counter this result. Billy did some more research. He concluded that removing his tongue would get him closer to being a true animatronic. He could still communicate, he learned, if he had a vocal synthesizer implanted in his throat. When Billy called Doc and explained what he wanted, Doc coughed and said, "Whatever you want."

Maliah, however, wasn't pleased with Billy's newest upgrade. She came over to see Billy the day he got back from Doc's, and she gasped when Billy opened his mouth and showed her the absence of his tongue.

"Why?" Maliah cried out.

To activate the synthesizer, Billy had to type his intended communication on his computer. "I no longer needed my tongue. A synthesizer is far preferable."

Maliah opened and closed her mouth. Then she burst into tears and ran out of Billy's house. He decided Maliah wasn't as satisfied as he was with his latest improvement.

The next day, Maliah called. "I'm very sorry I ran away," she said.

Billy typed in. "That is all right. You're just not capable

of understanding. It's not your fault. All humans are limited." He had almost typed in that he was an animatronic and he had to make the improvements he was making so he could be a better animatronic. But he couldn't go against his programming. Instead, he told her what he was going to have done next.

"Doc will be removing my ears next week," Billy said through his new synthesizer.

"What?" Maliah shrieked. "How will you hear?"

"I am only having the cartilage projecting from the sides of my head removed. My auditory sensors will remain intact."

"But you have nice ears," Maliah said.

"Ears are inconsistent with the essence of what I am," Billy said.

Maliah didn't speak. Billy could hear her breathing into the phone.

"Call me when you get back," she said quietly.

"I will do that," Billy said.

And he did. Maliah came over to see him the next day.

When she looked at him, Maliah chewed on her lower lip. "That doesn't look all that great now," she said as she glanced at the sutures cinching up Doc's incisions, "but after the hair grows back around them, it won't be all that noticeable."

"I want you to shave my head after the incisions heal," Billy said.

Maliah walked away from Billy and sat on the other side of the room. She stared at him for several seconds.

Finally, Maliah spoke. Her voice was unsteady. "Are you done now? Nothing else?"

Billy shook his head. "I am not done. I have some other unnecessary parts that need to be removed."

Maliah blinked. "Unnecessary parts," she repeated.

Billy nodded. He considered explaining the procedure to Maliah, but perhaps that was inadvisable.

Maliah stood. "I need to go, Billy."

Billy nodded. "All right."

Maliah walked over to Billy and tipped her head back as if she intended to kiss him. She closed her eyes and leaned toward him. Then she suddenly pulled back. She opened her eyes and stepped away. She lifted a hand to wave at him, and she left his house.

Billy didn't see Maliah anymore after that. He talked to her on the phone again, though. He called her the day he decided to change his name.

"Hi, Billy," Maliah said when he called. She didn't sound like she normally sounded. The way she sounded brought up an image from Billy's memory banks, an image of the way his mom had sounded in the days before her death.

"From now on," Billy said, "I would like to be called B-7. It's a name more in keeping with my true nature."

Maliah didn't respond. B-7 heard a click, and then he heard the phone's dial tone.

B-7 didn't call Maliah again until he had the last of his exterior changes done. A couple weeks after the last surgery, however, he picked up the phone and dialed her number.

"Hello?" Maliah answered.

"Hello, Maliah. It's B-7. I am calling to see if you would join me in the celebration of my sixteenth—what my mom would have said was my twenty-first—creation day. You can help me blow out candles."

Maliah was silent for a few seconds. Then she said, "I'm sorry, but I'm busy."

B-7 heard a click and the phone's dial tone.

On the morning of B-7's sixteenth (twenty-first) creation day, B-7 got up and prepared to put on his gray pants and gray shirt. Before he pulled them on, though, he felt compelled to go into his old room and look into the full-length mirror on the back of the door. He wanted to see the results of all the work he'd done to become consistent with his true self. He thought seeing the totality of his efforts would be a fitting way to celebrate the day.

When B-7 faced himself in the mirror, though, something quite surprising happened.

B-7 no longer wanted to have a celebration ritual.

Gazing at the prosthetics strapped to his four stumps, the bright red lumpy scars on his face and on the sides of his head where his ears used to be, the inky blackness of his eyes, and the tongueless maw of his mouth, B-7 got a sudden download of information. The download was system-wide, and it was shocking.

No, it was horrifying.

B-7 realized that he was not B-7.

Billy's prosthetic legs went out from under him. He

collapsed to the floor. He started to cry as he was overwhelmed by an avalanche of memories and realizations.

Mental images and sounds and words assaulted Billy, and the result completely reconfigured his perceptions. In a mind-blowing instant, Billy saw himself not as the ideal animatronic he'd been trying to be but as the complete failure of the man he'd now never be.

From deep inside Billy, a ragged wail erupted. The sound was guttural and garbled, but Billy more felt it than heard it. The keening tore up from within so violently that it felt like his emotions were trying to rip through his throat.

Billy had no one to comfort him as the self-image he'd held for sixteen years shattered around him. If his mom had still been here, she'd have hugged him and told him it was okay because he was her son. But she was gone. Maliah was gone, too.

Billy wriggled onto his side and curled himself into the tightest ball he could manage. He cringed at the way all his modifications prodded and poked at his remaining tender skin. It felt like every nerve ending in his body was on fire, screaming in rage and pain. His chest heaved. His heart pounded. His head was suddenly so pressurized that it felt like it was going to explode.

For a long time, Billy lay on the floor and struggled to breathe. He cried and he cried and he cried.

Eventually, his body couldn't produce any more tears. His breathing quieted. He was spent.

Billy stretched out his prosthetic legs and tried to

stand, but he couldn't. He had to crawl out of his old room and down the hall to his parents' bedroom.

Billy dragged himself over to the metal platform he'd been forcing himself to sleep on for so many years. The platform was cold and hard. Billy grabbed the edges of it and pulled himself upright.

Jerking across the room to the computer, Billy sat in his metal chair and linked his computer to his phone so he could use his synthesizer to communicate. Wiping his wet cube-shaped face with the back of his prosthetic hand, Billy called Doc.

"Can you undo what I've done?" Billy asked Doc.

Doc laughed so hard that he triggered a coughing fit, which went on for several seconds. Finally, he said. "Sorry, kid. No can do." Another of Doc's coughs racked him. When the cough ended, Doc spoke one last time. "Good luck, kid."

Doc hung up.

Billy set the phone down, but he didn't disconnect it. He let the dial tone buzz until the recorded voice urged him to hang up the phone. He ignored the voice until it went silent.

When the phone went silent, Billy didn't move. He couldn't move. All he could do was sit and stare straight ahead.

Billy wasn't aware of how long he sat and stared until he blinked and noticed the room was getting darker. He looked at the clock on his computer. He had been sitting in his chair for most of the day.

Painfully, Billy got up. He now knew what he needed to do.

Billy limped to his parents' closet. There, Billy pushed aside his own clothes and looked at the few clothes his dad hadn't taken when he'd left. Billy was the same size as his dad. He reached for a pair of his dad's jeans and one of his dad's shirts, a green one. After struggling into the clothes, Billy went out to the living room.

In the living room, Billy looked at the big plush gray sofa he hadn't used in years. The sofa was the same sofa his parents had sat on the night Billy had announced that he was an animatronic. Billy closed his eyes, and he could see his parents, side by side, behind his little five-year-old self.

Billy stumbled to the sofa and collapsed on it. It was soft, and it embraced him like no human arms ever would again.

Billy stayed on the sofa as the rest of the light faded from the day. He stayed on the sofa until the old dog across the street started barking. He stayed as dusk gave way to darkness. He stayed on the sofa for a while longer. Finally, Billy levered himself to his prosthetic feet. He walked to the front door and went out into the night.

Billy hadn't driven since his last limb amputation. He'd never been able to get his prosthetics to work together to operate the pedals and the steering wheel and the gear shift at the same time. He had, however, gotten better at walking.

Ungainly and faltering, Billy's walk was more of a herky-jerky wobble than a walk, but it moved him forward. So, Billy walked away from his house and headed down the sidewalk.

Billy didn't know what time it was now, but he knew it was late. No cars were moving on the streets. All the houses were dark but for the occasional porch light throwing long yellow glowing fingers across shadow-shrouded yards.

Thick gray clouds had descended on the town just before dusk, and they'd stayed. It was a moonless and starless night. The sky was a black tent pitched over the town.

Billy walked on.

He didn't know where he was going when he set out. All he'd been trying to do was get away from his life. He'd been attempting to escape the nightmare he'd created for himself.

When Billy reached where he was going, though, he realized it was the right place. It was the only place.

Billy walked up to the bent and rusted chain-link fence that surrounded his destination. His prosthetic hands gripped the links. He looked past the fence.

Beyond the fence lay the junkyard that Billy had gone past so many times, on his way to and from Doc's old mental hospital. The junkyard, now sitting in feeble light cast from a couple barely flickering security fixtures, was a place for discarded rubbish. Yes, this was the right place.

Billy followed the fence line for several feet, and he found a spot where the chain-link fence bulged outward. He turned sideways and wedged himself through the narrow opening.

Inside the fence, Billy started wandering up and down the rows of derelict vehicles and old battered appliances. At the end of one row, he spotted a station wagon similar to the one that still sat in his garage.

The station wagon was tucked into the metal enclosure of a car compactor. The enclosed space appealed to Billy. It looked like a little steel fort.

Billy veered toward the car. Grabbing the back door handle, Billy pulled on it. The rusted metal door caught and creaked in protest, but Billy was able to wrench it open. He crawled inside the car. And for the first time in sixteen years, Billy, the human, curled up on his side and went to sleep.

The clouds that had obscured the moon and the stars were gone when Billy woke up. At first, Billy thought the piercingly bright sun had awakened him, but then he realized that it wasn't light that had intruded into his sleep. It was sound . . . and vibration.

A loud engine was rumbling. Metal was crunching and pinging and snapping. And the station wagon was juddering as if caught in an earthquake.

Cringing, Billy raised his head just enough to peer through the dirty back window of the station wagon. Beyond the edge of the compactor's enclosure, a man stood at a control panel.

Before the man spotted Billy, Billy ducked his head down. He pressed himself against the station wagon's back seat. It was in a shadow. Billy didn't think anyone would see him there.

Billy closed his eyes and waited.

His wait wasn't long.

A humming roar began, and the station wagon's exterior began to crunch inward with a high-pitched metallic screech. Billy opened his eyes.

The station wagon's roof was coming down toward Billy. Even though Billy had feelings now because he was no longer an animatronic, the collapsing roof didn't upset him at all. In fact, he welcomed it. It was exactly what he wanted.

As the roof plunged downward, the roaring and screeching sounds amplified into a nearly deafening cacophony. The top of the station wagon compressed against Billy's body and then his skull.

The pain was excruciating . . . and it was complete. Every part of Billy screamed his humanity as the car caved inward on top of Billy. Billy opened his mouth to scream.

As Billy screamed, blood spurted from his mouth. For the first time, Billy welcomed the sight of his blood. It reminded him of who he really was. That reminder comforted him as his consciousness gave in and let go.

ABOUT THE AUTHORS

Scott Cawthon is the author of the bestselling video game series *Five Nights at Freddy's*, and while he is a game designer by trade, he is first and foremost a storyteller at heart. He is a graduate of the Art Institute of Houston and lives in Texas with his family.

Elley Cooper writes fiction for young adults and adults. She has always loved horror and is grateful whenever she can spend time in a dark and twisted universe. Elley lives in Tennessee with her family and many spoiled pets and can often be found writing books with Kevin Anderson & Associates.

Andrea Rains Waggener is an author, novelist, ghostwriter, essayist, short story writer, screenwriter, copywriter, editor, poet, and a proud member of Kevin Anderson & Associates' team of writers. In a past she prefers not to remember much, she was a claims adjuster, JCPenney's catalog order-taker (before computers!), appellate court clerk, legal writing instructor, and lawyer. Writing in genres that vary from her chick-lit novel, *Alternate Beauty*, to her dog how-to book, *Dog Parenting*, to her self-help book, *Healthy, Wealthy and Wise*, to ghostwritten memoirs to ghostwritten YA, horror, mystery, and mainstream fiction projects, Andrea still manages to find time to watch the rain and obsess over her dog and her knitting, art, and music projects. She lives with her husband and said dog on the Washington Coast, and if she isn't at home creating something, she can be found walking on the beach.

In a roiling auditory overload of screams and laughter, shouts and music, and bells and dings, one more shriek shouldn't have stood out. But this one did. Lucia stopped dead when she heard the shrill screech; it felt like the keen was spearing into her ears and drilling through her brain. All the hairs on the back of Lucia's neck stood up, and a shiver trickled down her spine. Her legs went weak.

Lucia looked toward the direction of the screech, up at the apex of the Zero Gravity ride. As she did, thick clouds that had been swallowing the night's stars for the last hour, gulped down the three-quarter moon, too. Suddenly, in spite of the carnival's thousands of glaring lights and the mild sixty-degree temperature, the night felt heavy and oppressive.

It was a bad omen. A very bad omen.

Lucia flinched when a hand gripped her upper arm.

She shook off the hand, took a step back, and forced herself to look. Jayce's face—her date's face (how weird was that, to be on a date?)—came into focus.

"Hey. Sorry," Jayce said. "You looked like you were going to faint or something. I was just trying to help. I didn't mean to . . ."

"It's okay," Lucia said. She dug deep and managed a smile she hoped didn't look as freaked as she felt.

I'm just on edge, Lucia told herself. She never would have chosen a carnival for a double date. A carnival wasn't just auditory overload; it was total sensory overload. Pressed by the crowd streaming through the midway, Lucia felt penned in by all the kaleidoscopic neon lights and garish colors of the spinning and whipping rides. And she cringed at the intrusive shouted chatter of the carnies who ran the games. Just a few feet away from Lucia, a tattooed man with a heavily creased face bellowed, "Three balls for a buck! Try your luck!"

Lucia liked quiet, not cacophony. She wasn't in her element.

But the screech that had disquieted Lucia was only a screech, one of hundreds emanating from the thrill rides. Thinking it was an omen was just her being "fanciful," something her logic-based parents would have scolded her for.

Lucia took a deep breath and started walking, knowing that Jayce would fall in step beside her. He was malleable, like an eager puppy.

When Lucia had stopped, she and Jayce had fallen behind their friends, Adrian and Hope. Zigging around a group of little kids arguing over cotton candy, Lucia scanned the crowded carnival midway and caught sight of Hope's bouncy strawberry blonde ponytail up ahead. Lucia could see dirty-blond curls a few inches above the ponytail. Even from this distance of twenty feet or so, even past the darting kids and sauntering teens and scattered families, Lucia could see the way Adrian's curls lay against the neck of his dark blue polo shirt, which fit him perfectly . . . as did his faded jeans. Or maybe she was just going from memory; Lucia could re-create the minutia of everything Adrian in her mind's eye. This wasn't a good thing. Adrian was her friend, not her boyfriend. He was with Hope. And now, thanks to Adrian's bizarre matchmaking efforts, Lucia was with Jayce.

Lucia walked faster. Jayce followed suit. They caught up with Adrian and Hope next to a funnel cake stand. Lucia inhaled the scent of fried dough and cinnamon. Somehow, the aromas managed to overpower all the other carnival scents—buttery popcorn, sizzling burgers, and sickly-sweet cotton candy; people's sweat and perfume; the rides' engine grease and sawdust. Lucia's nose was having to work overtime to keep up with all the olfactory input.

"I really shouldn't," Hope was saying as Adrian stepped up to a stainless-steel counter to order one of the oily, sugary things that Lucia thought looked like a dismembered donut that had been glued back together with oil.

Adrian turned and spotted Lucia and Jayce. "There you are. We thought we'd lost you. You want a funnel cake? I'm buying." Adrian flashed his perfect, white-toothed grin.

Lucia shook her head, but Jayce said, "Sure."

"Yo, dudes!" a deep voice boomed from behind them.

Lucia didn't bother to turn. She knew that voice. It belonged to Joel, the six-foot-six center on their school's basketball team.

"I had one of these funnel cakes last night," another deep voice said; this voice was crisper, filled with self-importance. "Eat at your own peril. I barfed mine up on the Orbiter ride."

Lucia sighed loudly as the two guys, both dressed in baggy jeans and team T-shirts in their school's unfortunate purple and gold colors, pushed past her. They each slapped Adrian on the back. He gave them a friendly smile, but Lucia knew Adrian well enough to know that he wasn't thrilled to see them. She didn't bother to smile at them. Why pretend you liked someone when you didn't?

"You must have decided to come at the last minute," Joel said to Adrian. He crossed his apelike arms in front of his barrel chest and cocked his big, bushy, sandy-haired head. "And you lost your phone so you couldn't call and let us know." He elbowed Wade, the self-professed barfer. "Think we're not welcome?"

Wade grinned. "Oh, sure we are. The more the merrier. Right, Hope?" He winked at Hope.

Hope gave Wade a stiff smile and took Adrian's arm. Wade nonchalantly ran a hand through his long brown hair as if Hope's lack of interest didn't bother him. His narrowed brown eyes and stiff thin lips gave away his true feelings.

Lucia had an odd moment of empathy for Wade. She didn't like him, but she could relate to how he felt. Wade, who thought he was the king of their class and all girls should treat him accordingly, had wanted to date Hope for years. He probably thought it was his right to date her. He was the celebrated quarterback of the football team, the head jock in the school, and Hope was the head cheerleader. Lucia was sure that in Wade's mind, he and Hope were royalty; they should have been together. But even though she was a statuesque cheerleader, almost supermodel beautiful with five feet, four inches of athletic curves, shining hair, and big cartoon-princess eyes and rosy lips, Hope wasn't stuck-up and elitist like Wade was. She was actually very nice. And she was with six-foot-two sculpted Adrian, the star of the school's basketball team. Adrian was also one of the senior class "royalty," but he didn't think of himself that way.

Adrian was the reason why Lucia's senior year was going a lot better than she'd thought it would when she and her parents had moved to the town just before her last year of high school. Given that she was a straight-A student, a science and tech geek with an incongruous obsession with the supernatural, and not at all interested in looking and acting "normal," Lucia figured she'd be an outcast. But she wasn't . . . because she and her family happened to move across the street from Adrian, a nice guy who made sure Lucia felt welcomed and included.

Lucia watched Adrian's friendly blue eyes crinkle as he accepted a tray of funnel cakes and began passing them around. He was so gorgeous—his face belonged on magazine covers; Lucia never tired of watching him, except when her wish that he was more than a friend was too much for her.

"Hey, Hope! Are you really eating fried bread? Shame on you!" Nick, one of the five males on their high school's cheerleading squad, came up behind Hope and bumped her good-naturedly.

A tall, slender girl who looked like she was trying to be invisible trailed behind Nick. Hope smiled at her. "Hey, Kel. I didn't know you guys were coming here tonight."

The girl shrugged. She looked at the group and then dropped her gaze to her feet.

Hope, who had just taken her first bite of funnel cake, quickly wiped sugar and grease off her lips. She chewed, then giggled. "Join me for a couple extra laps in the morning?" she asked Nick. "I'll have to work this off."

"Only if you share," Nick said. He reached out and pulled off a piece of Hope's funnel cake.

"Take as much as you want," Hope said. She looked past Nick. "You want some, Kel?"

Kel—Kelly to everyone except Hope—blinked and shook her head as she toyed with her long, brown single braid. *Poor Kelly*, Lucia thought. Kelly was so excruciatingly shy when she was in groups. She was Hope's best friend (or one of them—Hope was close friends with Nick, too), and she was a nice girl, bright and funny. Kelly wasn't a cheerleader. Apparently, she and Hope had been friends since they were in kindergarten together. Lucia had overheard Kelly when she thought she was alone with Hope or Nick. Kelly had a lot of interesting things to say because she genuinely liked to study and she read all the time. Pretty, with exotically slanted hazel eyes and soft, freckled features, Kelly dressed well—if you were into current fashions. Tonight, she wore ankle-hugging olive pants with a cropped tan top that revealed her flat stomach. Lucia wondered what had happened to Kelly to steal her self-confidence.

"Kelly and I just gorged on corn dogs, popcorn, and milkshakes." Nick snatched another piece of Hope's funnel cake. He opened his wide mouth and popped in the bite. The sugar that remained on his lower lip made him look like a little boy, but then, his soft, smooth features always gave him a boyish look. Green-eyed, ginger-haired Nick was cute in a kid-next-door kind of way.

"And you're still eating," Hope said affectionately.

Nick chewed and swallowed. "But of course. My muscles need fuel." He struck a bodybuilder pose, and Hope laughed.

Although he wasn't a jock, Nick's muscles rivaled the bulging brawn of Joel and Wade. Adrian was ripped, too, but in a less in-your-face way. He was just fit, not muscle-bound.

Jayce nudged Lucia, startling her. She whipped her head toward him. Oh yeah, her date. She forced a smile and shook her head at the piece of fried dough he offered her. It didn't look appetizing in the least. All lumpy and shiny and tangled—it reminded her of intestines. Another shiver rippled through her. She put her back to Jayce and the others and turned to watch the roller-coaster cars clatter past on their downward swoop into a loop-the-loop that jutted out fifty feet above the roof of the funnel cake stand.

"So now what?" Joel asked as the whole group moved on and eventually clustered at the edge of the Balloons and Darts game. Lucia joined the others, her gaze on the dart-throwing kids standing at the game's counter. She mentally calculated the optimal trajectory that would pop the uppermost red balloon. She could visualize the perfect arc in her head.

"We've been on all the rides and played most of the games," Hope said. She grinned up at Adrian adoringly. "We had to walk back to his truck to leave all the prizes he won for me."

Adrian didn't react to the praise. He was too humble to be cocky about his game prowess. He concentrated on eating his funnel cake.

Wade rolled up onto the balls of his feet and puffed out his chest. "I won a bunch of stuff last night, so I didn't even bother to play tonight. Joel and I just wanted to go on the rides again."

Lucia rolled her eyes. As if, she thought. If Wade won anything, it was probably one of the little rubber duck prizes they gave out at the Duck Pond game. Wade wasn't nearly as awesome as he thought he was.

How did I get here? Lucia wondered. She didn't even like carnivals.

But what could she do when Adrian told her he'd set up the double date? He was being nice, and she'd figured saying no would have been rude. And it wasn't like she didn't like Jayce. He was a nice guy, too.

Jayce was Adrian's unlikely best friend. Unlikely because Jayce was the antithesis of a jock. About five foot, six inches and skinny, Jayce looked like the consummate nerd. He had thick black hair that was never properly combed, equally thick, black-rimmed round glasses that he constantly had to push back up on his nose, and a pale angular face that couldn't be called good-looking by anyone, probably not even his mother. On top of his unfortunate looks, Jayce dressed in checked dress shirts paired with dress slacks, and he always had at least a dozen pens and pencils stuffed into a pocket protector. He looked like he was the male version of Lucia, a science nerd, but he wasn't all that bright. He was more creative than intelligent. Jayce was an artist, a pretty brilliant one actually. He could draw and paint the most amazing portraits. He'd done one of Lucia that had made her look downright pretty.

Without Jayce's artistic talents to help her, Lucia wouldn't have described herself as pretty. She'd always thought her face was too thin and angular to be attractive. She also had odd features—one eye was much bigger than the other, her nose was slightly crooked, and her mouth was too wide for her face. All this was part of a head she thought was too big for her petite five-foot-two frame—accentuated by her wild, kinky black curls, which she could never fully contain but didn't have the heart to chop off. Lucia's late grandmother had loved Lucia's afro-like hair; so, Lucia let her hair radiate from her head like a black nimbus in honor of her beloved nana. Her clothes were a tribute to her nana, too. Lucia had a closet full of woven vests in a variety of colors and patterns, all handcrafted by Nana; Lucia paired these vests with men's black shirts, ankle-length skirts, and hiking boots. Even under the protection of Adrian's friendship, Lucia's wardrobe raised eyebrows on a regular basis.

A kid eating a slice of pizza walked past, bumping into Wade. "Hey," Wade said. "Watch where you're going."

The kid, who looked to be ten or so, stuck out his pizza-sauce-covered tongue at Wade and ran off. Wade looked as if he was going to give chase, but before he could, Joel grabbed his arm.

"I've got a great idea," Joel said loudly. He turned and pointed past the roller coaster, toward the dome-shaped metal skeleton of Freddy Fazbear's Mega Pizzaplex. "Let's go over there and look around."

Lucia gazed toward the well-lit construction site. She shivered.

The town had been buzzing about the massive entertainment center for months, ever since Fazbear Enterprises announced its intention to create a coliseum-size arena filled with games, rides, restaurants, and stages that would feature all the Fazbear animatronic characters. Everyone thought the project was wonderful; it was an economic boon for the town. It was supposed to create tons of new jobs and bring in thousands of tourists. Lucia wasn't so sure the place was a great idea. She'd read stories about the old Freddy Fazbear pizzerias. There were rumors, dark ones. She'd even heard that the pizzeria was being built over the top of one of those pizzerias with a checkered past.

"Why would we go over there?" Hope asked. "It's just a construction site."

"Yeah, but it's a good one. I've checked it out a couple times. Now I hear they've already started bringing in animatronics," Joel said. "Maybe we can find one and get it turned on or something."

"Maybe we'll get arrested and go to jail," Jayce said.

Joel curled his thick upper lip and looked down at Jayce. "You a scaredy-cat, runt?"

"Joel," Adrian said, "knock it off."

Jayce stepped forward and put his shoulders back. "It's okay, Adrian. I got this." He pushed his glasses up on his nose and tilted his head back so he could look Joel in the eye. "Just because I'm small and I draw doesn't mean I'm a scaredy-cat, you neanderthal."

"Wanna bet?" Joel poked Jayce in the chest. "I bet if we go over there and we find one of those animatronics, you'll pee your pants."

"I don't know if going over there is such a good idea," Nick spoke up. "I heard something weird happened not that long ago, something hush-hush."

"Great!" Joel said. "A mystery. Let's make like Scooby-Doo and the gang and go solve it. What do you say, dudes?"

Lucia opened her mouth to say she wanted to go home, but she never got the words out because Kelly—big shock—spoke up. "I like mysteries. I just read a book on urbex . . . urban exploration. It would be cool to poke around an old site."

Joel raised an unruly eyebrow and looked at Kelly as if he was seeing her in a new light. "Now, that's the spirit."

"I'm in," Jayce said.

Lucia took his hand and leaned over so she could whisper in his ear. "You don't have to prove anything."

Jayce whispered back, "Yes, I do. If you don't stand up to them, they end up pounding you down."

"But Adrian won't let that happen," Lucia persisted.

"Adrian isn't always going to be around to fight my battles," Jayce said.

Adrian looked at Jayce as if he'd overheard the comment. "Are you sure, Jayce?" he asked. "We can just leave."

Jayce nodded. "I'm sure. Let's do it."

Adrian's sculpted nose twisted as he thought. He looked down at Hope. "What do you say? Are you willing to go over there?"

Hope's big blue eyes shifted from Joel to Jayce and back again. She wasn't stupid. She understood the dynamic at play. She looked over at Kelly. "Do you really want to go over there?"

Kelly flushed and wrapped the end of her braid around her fingers, but she nodded. When she spoke, her words were barely audible. "It could be fun."

"Or not," Lucia muttered.

Kelly's eyes flickered. She obviously heard Lucia, but she didn't say anything else.

"Then let's blow this carnival and go have some fun," Joel said. He threw an arm around Wade and began pulling his friend along the midway.

Nick looked at Hope and Adrian, his full cheeks sucked in as if in deep thought. Adrian gestured at Jayce. "Your call."

"Let's go," Jayce said.

Lucia couldn't help but notice that her date hadn't asked her what she wanted. Should she call it a night and head home on her own? She shrugged. No, she had to admit the idea of finding an animatronic kind of appealed to her. She was fascinated by robotics.

So, Lucia followed her friends and her not-friends through the carnival revelers. She tried not to think about the screech that had unnerved her earlier.

***

The Pizzaplex construction site waited, still and silent, in the mottled shadows cast between sporadically spaced security lights. Surrounded by a twelve-foot chain-link fence that was plastered with DANGER—DO NOT ENTER signs, the construction site looked, at first glance, to be out of reach. But Joel knew how to get in.

"There's some loose fencing down this way," he said, leading the group to the side of the site farthest from the carnival.

It had taken just ten minutes for them to walk from the carnival to the construction site, but it took another ten to circumnavigate the unfinished domed structure because the fencing was set a hundred yards or so beyond the edges of the building itself. Lucia gazed past the chain-link barrier as they traipsed over the dusty earth extending from the fence. Within the fencing, Lucia could see the hulking shapes of a couple dump trucks and excavators. A crane's boom extended toward the metal skeleton of the unfinished dome. It looked like a giant robotic arm was reaching out, searching for a connection.

Isn't that what we're all doing? Lucia thought. Lucia looked around at the others. They were all here because they were trying to connect, trying to be part of something, even if they would never admit it . . . not even to themselves.

Lucia's rubber-soled boots made hushed scuffling sounds as she walked. Hope's dainty sandals sounded like tap shoes. The others' athletic shoes chuffed at the earth. Occasionally, someone would kick a piece of gravel, and it would ping off the metal fencing.

In the distance, they could hear the over-the-top gaiety of the carnival but it was strangely muted, as if the construction site acted as a sound dampener. Lucia could no longer smell all the carnival aromas. Now, all her nose detected was the arid smell of the earth and a sharp whiff of gasoline.

Joel suddenly stopped, and so did everyone else. He reached out and tugged at a section of fencing. With a metallic scrape, it pulled back from one of the fence's metal poles. "Here we go," Joel said.

No one responded to him. They just slithered, single-file, through the opening. As Lucia squeezed through, a sharp chain-link edge scraped against the back of her wrist. She winced at the sudden pain. She couldn't see the cut, but warmth trickling down the back of her hand let her know the skin was broken, though not seriously. She pulled down the sleeve of her black shirt to staunch the flow.

Nick was the last one through the fence. As he let the chain-link fall back into place with a twang that made Lucia stiffen, he looked around worriedly. "Are you sure there are no dogs?" Nick asked.

Joel shook his head. He waved an arm toward the Pizzaplex. "I've been all over the site. No dogs. No guards." He pointed to a spot about a hundred feet away. "There are some security cameras over there, near the office trailer and the construction materials, but we don't need to get anywhere near them to see inside the dome."

Lucia gazed at the piles of rebar and stacks of metal beams. Beyond them, a cement truck sat, it's mixing drum bulging like it was pregnant. Lucia's imagination suddenly provided her with a vision of alien insectoid-like nanobots pouring from the mixing drum. She blinked and mentally chastised herself. The deserted site was creepy enough without her brain adding to it.

No one spoke as Joel led the way past a steamroller to an opening between two half-finished cement walls. "There's an enclosure just past here. I think that's where the animatronics are being stored."

Thankfully, more security lights were set up within the unfinished structure. The metal floodlights didn't flood so much as they spurted into darkness here and there, but they provided enough visibility to get around . . . and enough visibility to reveal a flat, red metal roof surrounded by the concrete floor Lucia and the others now stood on.

"Is that the roof of the old pizzeria?" Kelly asked.

Lucia was again surprised to hear Kelly speak up. But, gazing at Kelly's wide eyes, Lucia could tell Kelly was really excited, so excited that she'd apparently forgotten to be shy.

"What pizzeria?" Hope asked. She was clinging to Adrian's arm. She obviously didn't want to be here, but she was trying to be a good sport.

"It's an old Freddy Fazbear pizzeria site," Lucia said. "I read about it. I think they're going to turn it into a museum or something."

"Look over there," Nick said. "There's a ramp that looks like it's heading down, maybe toward the pizzeria's entrance."

"Come on." Joel's shadow stretched twelve feet ahead of him as he started toward the ramp Nick had pointed out. "I never noticed that when I was here before."

Their footsteps crackled and echoed as they all followed Joel toward the ramp. When they got closer to it, though, they realized the ramp led to nowhere. A couple feet down the ramp's slope, it ended at a bulging mass of hardened concrete that swelled in a knobby mass from somewhere farther down the slope.

"We're not getting in that way," Wade said. He started to turn away.

"That's the worse concrete pour I've ever seen," Adrian said. He moved down the ramp, leaned over, and poked at the clot of cement.

"Maybe it was a spill," Jayce said.

Adrian shook his head. "I don't know." He frowned then shrugged. "It's just weird is all."

"Hey, look," Wade called from a few feet away. Everyone turned.

Wade pointed toward the far side of the flat red roof. "Come on. I think I see a vent opening that might be big enough to get through."

Wade trotted a few feet to their left and stepped from the Pizzaplex's concrete floor to the corrugated surface of the red metal roof. His feet grated against the uneven surface as he landed. When he started striding across the red metal, the cadence of his steps echoed through the dim enclosure of the fledgling Pizzaplex. The rhythm became uneven and chaotic as everyone else followed him.

About fifty feet from the blocked-off ramp, Wade knelt next to a square metal protrusion. Gripping its edges, he yanked . . . and it easily came free; he lost his balance and landed on his butt.

Jayce chuckled. Joel turned and glared.

Wade didn't seem to care about Jayce's amusement. He immediately got to his knees and grabbed the steel vent grating that the metal square had concealed. It didn't come free easily, but when Wade jiggled it back and forth several times, it groaned and grumbled, and finally, with a loud snap, let go of the roof. Beneath the grate, a narrow, dark chute led downward.

Wade immediately stuck his feet into the chute. He looked up at the others and grinned. "Ready for an adventure?"

"I'm not going down into that hole," Hope said. "We don't know where it goes."

"That's the fun of a mystery," Kelly spoke up.

Lucia mentally shook her head. Kelly was surprising Lucia right and left tonight.

Wade looked at Kelly with interest. "That a girl," he said.

Joel reached into his pocket and pulled out a tiny flashlight. He shone it down the chute.

They all leaned forward to peer into the chute. The light didn't help them much. It revealed a narrow metal enclosure slanting downward toward a bend that hid whatever lay beyond it.

"Give me that." Wade reached for Joel's flashlight.

Joel shrugged and gave up the light. "Okay. Lead on. I'll be right behind you."

Wade slid feetfirst into the chute. Joel did the same. Within seconds, they both disappeared around the bend.

An anemic beam of light managed to make it back up to Lucia and the others as Wade's and Joel's progress was marked by metallic thuds and clanks. A few more seconds of that noise passed. Then they heard a muted thump and a loud "Ouch!" "Whoa, dude," Joel said, his voice echoing up the chute.

Adrian and Hope exchanged a concerned look.

Lucia rubbed the goose bumps on her arms. She glanced around at the Pizzaplex's vast darkened expanse.

"You guys need to get down here!" Joel called out. "This is seriously dope!"

Kelly crouched down and quickly slid down the chute as Hope called out, "Kel!"

More thuds and clanks. An "oof" and then Wade said, "I've got you! Great job, Kelly!"

Hope leaned over the opening in the roof. "Are you okay, Kel?"

"I'm fine." Kelly's voice sounded tinny and distant, but her eager excitement was obvious. "It really is wicked down here. You need to see this."

Hope looked at Adrian. "I hate to leave Kelly down there alone with those two."

Adrian released a resigned breath. "I agree. Let me go first."

Hope nodded.

And that was when Lucia and the others lost their minds.

What do you do when five of your group of eight have already charged into the breach? Do you retreat, looking like a total wuss? For Jayce and Nick, the answer was a resounding no. Lucia had to think a little harder but not for long. Adrian was down there.

★★★

When Lucia slid out the vent chute, Jayce did his best to catch her. His best wasn't great, unfortunately, and the two of them ended up tumbling across the floor together. They landed next to a stack of old, sagging cardboard boxes. Lucia's long skirt tangled around Jayce's shoulders. She quickly whipped it free and smoothed it over her legs.

"I think we're in the storage room," Kelly said. "There's a hallway out here." She pointed. "I'm pretty sure it leads to the dining room."

Jayce immediately popped to his feet and offered Lucia his hand. "Sorry about that," he said.

Lucia smiled at him. "No problem."

She suddenly realized how well she could see.

Although the light that surrounded her was dim, it was adequate to reveal that she and the others were now in a red-walled room filled with old boxes. They had to be in a Freddy Fazbear's pizzeria. Even in the shadows, she could see the infamous black-and-white checkered floor.

She could also see piles of metal endoskeleton parts. Mounds of robotic arms and legs and torsos and skulls were strewn through the space, along with the boxes.

"I'm surprised there are lights down here," Hope said. She was brushing a smudge of dirt off the pale-yellow blouse she wore with her tight jeans.

"They must have piggybacked the power from the Pizzaplex construction lights," Adrian said.

"Come on," Joel said. "Kelly's right. The dining room's down there." He pointed.

Joel started down the hall, his footsteps heavy and loud. The others followed him. Lucia took up the rear.

Within seconds, the group stepped into a big room filled with more endoskeleton parts. These were scattered among broken tables and chairs and a few brightly-colored plastic plates and purple-striped tablecloths.

"What's that smell?" Lucia asked.

The odor had hit her the minute she'd landed on the floor in the storage room, and she hadn't thought much about it. You'd expect an old buried restaurant to smell dank and musky. But now the stench seemed to be getting stronger.

"It smells like something dead," Nick said. "Maybe a rat."

Hope squeaked and pressed against Adrian. He pulled her close as he gazed around the room. "What happened down here?" he asked. "Why are all these robotic parts all over?"

Jayce started poking around. Metal clacked against metal as he picked up parts and shifted them. "Maybe they're using the place as a storage area until they get the rest of the Pizzaplex built."

"Yeah, but why are they storing old, broken robotic parts?" Lucia asked.

Adrian let go of Hope. Clearly curious, he, too, began looking around. Hope hugged herself and pressed back against the edge of a small semicircular stage, which was next to a long, rectangular one. *The small stage would have been Foxy's stage,* Lucia thought. The animatronic fox had been a fixture in the old Freddy Fazbear pizzerias.

Lucia left Hope and joined the others. Jayce had pulled out his small sketch pad and was drawing a robotic skull. The rest of the group was traipsing through the robotic rubble, shifting a metal arm here, a metal leg there. Lucia's gaze shifted from part to part to part. The heads were the most unsettling parts. Their dead eyes . . .

Lucia stopped and stared.

She realized that the head she was looking at wasn't made of metal.

It wasn't an animatronic head.

It was . . .

Lucia stumbled back and covered her mouth. The burger she and Jayce had shared at the start of the evening churned in her stomach. She turned and threw it up.

Jayce was at her side immediately. "Lucia! What . . ."

Lucia, so chilled she felt like she'd stepped into a freezer, lifted a shaking finger. She pointed at the head that was still lying on its side, its clouded eyes staring. She opened her mouth, but she couldn't get a word out.

Jayce looked in the direction of Lucia's finger. He frowned and stepped toward the head, shoving his sketch pad back in his pocket. "Is that some kind of prop?" He leaned over and touched the head.

He yelped and fell, landing on his hands and knees. He started scrabbling away from the head.

At the same time, Kelly let out a scream even more ear-splitting than the one Lucia had heard at the carnival. And because Kelly's scream wasn't entangled with other screams and carnival sounds, it pierced through the silence like a scythe.

Lucia and Jayce, already shocked, had to struggle to their feet before they could head toward Kelly. Everyone else, even Hope, was at Kelly's side in an instant.

In that same moment, Hope's screams joined Kelly's. The guys' gasps were the base to the girls' soprano cries.

Lucia and Jayce finally reached the others. Reluctantly, Lucia looked in the direction of their gazes. And she blanched. Her stomach flipped over again. She gagged but managed to keep from heaving.

Piled together in a macabre pyramid, a gruesome tangle of human limbs, torsos, and heads were rotting next to a snarl of ragged metal endoskeleton parts. Lucia, unconsciously, did an inventory of the parts; at least eleven bodies were lumped together, in pieces.

Lucia's brain—against her will—took in the details. The severed heads and dismembered arms and legs hadn't been cut away from the limbless torsos. The ends of the exposed bones were jagged; they'd been snapped, not sawed through. Torn tissue and mangled veins revealed the same thing. These bodies had been wrenched apart. What could do that?

Unable to look away from the savagery, Lucia noticed dark, rust-colored stains sprayed across the floor and the walls. Dried blood was everywhere, even spotting the metal robotic parts.

Adrian recovered himself first. He grabbed Hope's hand and pulled her back from the grisly heap. "We need to get out of here."

No one argued with him. When Adrian turned, everyone followed him. They all ran back across the dining room, pounding into the hallway and scrambling past the boxes in the storage room.

There, however, they all stopped. The bottom of the chute was no longer open. The metal had collapsed, crushed together as if crimped by a giant hand. Their escape route was blocked.

Everyone stared at the closed-off chute. They panted in unison and exchanged wide-eyed, pale-faced looks.

Adrian was the first to get a grip. "There has to be another way out. Come on."

Adrian led the group down the hallway away from the dining room. The hallway ended at an exit door, but the door was engulfed in cement blocks and more robotic parts.

"Help me." Adrian squatted next to a cement block. He and the other guys tried to lift it. It wouldn't budge.

Adrian stood and took a deep breath. "Okay. There have to be other doors. Windows. Something."

And there were other doors. And windows. But they were all blocked. Some were actually cemented closed. Nothing would open. Nothing would give way, no matter how much effort the guys put into it. And a search of the entire restaurant didn't reveal any other vertical chutes. It also didn't reveal any tools that would have helped them pry apart the closed-off chute. Adrian suggested they use robotic arms to try and peel back the metal blocking their egress, but his idea didn't work.

They were trapped.

Unwilling to return to the dining room, where the decaying body parts seemed to pulse with malevolent intent, the group started down the hall leading to the storage room. Their footsteps made skirring sounds as they all shuffled, flat-footed in defeat, over the grit-covered floor.

By now, they were all dirty and sweaty and breathing heavily. Lucia hadn't stopped shaking since she'd seen the first head.

Adrian put his arm around Hope. "Don't worry. When the construction crew returns in the morning, we'll hear them. We can bang on the metal and they're sure to hear us. They'll get us out."

Hope gave Adrian a little hesitant nod that belied her name. Trailing behind the couple, Lucia wished Adrian would put his arm around her, too. Maybe reading—or misreading—her thoughts, Jayce sidled close and took Lucia's hand; she didn't protest.

About halfway down the hallway, Adrian stopped. He held up a hand. "Listen," he whispered.

They clustered around Adrian as he turned back toward the way they'd just come. As soon as their steps ceased, they heard it . . . a creak. Everyone strained to see into the dimness of the dining room.

The creak sounded again, loudly. Now, it was an unmistakable creak, a creak of moving metal.

"What is that?" Joel asked.

"Shh," Adrian said. He cocked his head to listen.

The creak repeated itself. It sounded like a metal gate swinging back and forth in a breeze . . . sort of. It was an odd sound. The creak was caught up in a faint hiss.

Adrian pressed his lips together the way he always did when he was thinking deeply. He looked at the others. "Come on. Let's go check it out." He didn't whisper, but he kept his voice low. "It sounds like it might be a vent cover, maybe a ventilation system? Might be a way out."

Lucia frowned, but she didn't say anything. The desire for the sound to lead to a way out was stronger than her intuition that the sound wasn't anything as benign as a ventilation system.

They took a few paces toward the dining room. Without discussing it, everyone stepped lightly, as quietly as possible. Lucia listened hard. The others must have been listening hard, too, because when the sound changed, they all stopped as one.

The creak beyond the doorway to the dining room

gave way to a series of footstep-like taps, followed by another metallic creak, entwined with a long hiss and a rasp.

The sounds were getting closer. Each tap brought the hissing creak nearer to the hallway.

Hope clutched Adrian's arm. Lucia held her breath.

A clunk came from just a few feet beyond the doorway.

Adrian grabbed Hope's hand and started running back down the hall toward the storage room. Hope went along without question. So did everyone else.

Lucia's heart was lurching up toward her throat as they all tore into the storage room. She was sure the others could hear the pounding beats thumping against her rib cage.

As soon as they were all through the door, Adrian closed the door quietly . . . and locked it.

Everyone stared at the door.

"What if it's someone coming to help us?" Wade whispered.

The very fact that he whispered revealed the doubt behind his words.

The others didn't answer the question. They just looked at one another with wide eyes. Clearly, everyone was realizing what Lucia had known as soon as she'd heard the first creak.

They weren't down here alone.

And whatever was down here with them wasn't here to help them get out.